*Sealskin Trousers*
*and other stories*

*By the same author*

SQUARE PEG (a novel)
SO SAY BANANA BIRD (a novel)
MARVELLOUS PARTY (a play)
A PINCH OF SALT (a play)
THE CIVILISED ALTERNATIVE
FOOD FOR A FUTURE
THE EXTENDED CIRCLE (editor)
ANYTHING WITHIN REASON (a novel)

# *Sealskin Trousers*
## *and other stories*

Jon Wynne-Tyson

OAKROYD PRESS

First published in Great Britain 1994
by Oakroyd Press, 9 Oakroyd Avenue,
Potters Bar, Hertfordshire EN6 2EH

A CIP catalogue record for this title is
available from the British Library

ISBN 0 9512210 2 7

With acknowledgements to *Between the Species* (USA); *Etica &
Animali* (Italy); *Literary Review* (UK); *Night Cry* (USA); *Omni*
(USA); *The Twilight Zone* (USA); *The Year's Best Horror Stories*
(USA).

Typeset by
Willow-Type, East Dean, Sussex PO18 0JB
Printed and bound by
Antony Rowe Ltd., Chippenham, Wiltshire SN14 6QA

# Contents

For Oliver, William, Matthew, Victoria, Giles
and Toby, readers of stories.

# Sealskin Trousers

IT WAS a success story all right. Rags to rags and riches, so to speak. No-one had expected it of young Sol Singer, least of all his parents living out the tail end of their sad lives in the dampest corner of Canning Town, within smelling range of Bow Creek where it crawls darkly into the Thames.

Agreed, Sol might have had the odd wild brief dream of one day owning his own firm, but when in 1947 he was taken on as trainee cutter at Bertelman of Margaret Street, smack bang in the rag trade quarter of London's West End, he thought himself lucky to have any work at all at a time when most of the jobs were going to the lately demobbed. It certainly never crossed his mind he would one day be able to make a serious bid for the mighty firm of Ebenezer Bertelman and Co., Ltd., later Inc., which is what he did.

He sometimes wondered whether it would have happened at all if, about a year after he started work there, old man Bertelman had not been visited by a salesman peddling subscriptions to a monthly American trade fashion magazine. Full of glossy colour work it was, mostly advertisements, teasing a luxury-hungry post-war Britain with what the *haute monde* of less exhausted countries had begun to take for granted again. To Sol it was a treasure house of ideas and opportunities. Each time the latest number of *Fur Fashions* arrived, he would smuggle back to his squalid East End room the last issue but two. That way old Bertelman never missed any.

1

But the nuts and bolts of success stories can be rather a yawn except to their central characters, so suffice it that by the early 1950s young Sol had started up on his own, and within very few years, hardly pausing to swallow up the no longer spunky Ebenezer Bertelman and Co. Ltd. (the old man had never really paid much attention to *Fur Fashions*, which maybe is relevant), he was one of the most respected names among London's furriers. His sumptuous premises were a mere stone's throw to the east of Broadcasting House, and his splendid neo-Georgian mansion in Bishop's Avenue, N2, was within a further and even shorter throw of Ken Wood, that most prestigious of all portions of Hampstead Heath.

Long before that, of course, he had married Miriam, not only because she had useful connections including an immensely wealthy New York father, but also because she was a dark, flashing, intelligent beauty of a woman and (let's be honest about this) a cut or two above Sol in the social scheme of things.

Between them, as might be supposed, they produced children: Louis, Edna, Benjamin, and finally Irina (for Miriam had some Russian blood). These they reared with a realistic devotion often conspicuously absent in their wealthy western goy counterparts, and when each had made good in his or her turn and had multiplied success-fully, the hearts of Sol and Miriam were full indeed.

Louis and Benjamin, of course, went into their father's business. Edna and Irina, both as beautiful as their mother, if not as sharply intelligent, did what she did, which was to marry well if not better.

All of which goes to prove that single-mindedness pays. Never for one moment had either Sol or Miriam indulged in those sloppy liberal sentiments beloved of the British and American middle classes who have read the right books and Sunday supplements and fall over backwards to rear their offspring without beliefs or inhibitions, and so in most cases with minimal sense of purpose or obligation.

2

Had he been born into a less closely-knit family, Louis, the eldest, might have become a distinguished academic or man of letters. He was a very serious person, inclined to write unstaged plays reminiscent of Ibsen's, but without the laughs. But with his head for figures and his firm but fair way with people, it was soon accepted that he would be wasted in any role but that of successor to his father.

Benjamin . . . well, Benjamin might have been a problem had he received less parental attention from the first moment his character began to show itself. He was a very different cup of tea to Louis, much more extroverted and physical; puzzlingly so to Sol and Miriam whose disinclination for bodily exertion was such that conservation of physical energy had been a lifelong priority.

"Benny," his father had said when the boy was in his early twenties, "do not think I am unreasonably criticising you, but I cannot see for why you must squander yourself hitting balls in a squash court. There is more to life than playing unproductive games."

"I know that, father, but a desk and a telephone don't stretch me. I need something more to get my adrenalin flowing."

"Ah, ah!" his mother had said, nodding vigorously. "It is his grandfather coming through."

Sol could respect this judgment, for Miriam's father's fortune had been made at the rougher end of the fashion business, out on the ice and in the great northern forests of the New World where in his early years the beasts were there for clubbing, shooting and trapping by any prepared to face the hardships and uncertainties of making a living by transferring the pelts of wild creatures to the backs of submissive women. In those halcyon times fashion had not become a political issue. There was no threat from the conservationist lobbies that to-day bedevil the freedom of those whose uncomplicated ambition is to bring into another's life the beauty inherent in furry key rings, toy animals, bikinis, lavatory seat covers, handbags, bedside

3

rugs, and the other essentials of the civilised *dolce vita*. The first principle of a democratic consumer society, that demand justifies supply, was as fresh and untarnished as the day it was conceived.

Schooled in this great tradition, Benjamin was encouraged to keep his feet in two camps, those of his father and of his maternal grandfather. He worked with as much enthusiasm for the latter as for the former, not only in the London and New York offices but out on the Arctic ice where he never felt more fulfilled than when stretched to his physical limits clubbing the seals that had so usefully contributed to his grandfather's fortune. The rugged outdoor atmosphere of Canada and North America was more to his liking than the softer options of England, though his wife Jackie, a Londoner born and bred, had long since steered his mind away from any ambition to make their main home outside the U.K. So Jackie and their four adorable little girls lived in Golders Green, only a mile or so from Sol and Miriam.

For some time before retirement Sol had been resigned to the habit of the long week-end. It is not easy for a workaholic to know what to do with a long week-end in the absence of any burning interest in physical recreation, spectator sportsmanship, country house viewing, art, music or serious reading. But the summer months at least were no problem, for Benjamin kept a powerful motor vessel in a wide natural harbour an easy Rolls drive from North London, and he and Miriam between them had persuaded Sol that few things could be better for himself and the grandchildren than regular acquaintance with sea air.

It was good psychology. Sol was devoted to Rebecca, Jacintha, Paula and Miranda, if only marginally more than to his six other grandchildren whom distance made less accessible, and it was a frequent summer treat to drive them to the bleak east coast inlet where a small but attentive boatyard looked after "Sea Pirate".

4

"Sea Pirate," for those unschooled in such matters, was a huge triple-decked box of a boat, forty feet overall and high out of the water, lavishly appointed with a king-size bed in the owner's cabin, a sumptuous bathroom, a dream galley, and packed with a wealth of technology from autopilot, radio telephone, air conditioning, central heating, bar and icemaker to the latest in marine audio communication systems. Powerful twin diesel engines pushed this floating playground through the water at improbable speeds, and a fearsome sight she could be when plunging at twenty knots and more through choppy seas, bristling with long whip radio and TV aerials, radar and other equipment, from a soaring tuna tower above the flying-bridge to rods and winches for catching and landing everything from a careless mackerel to the deep-sea game fish for whose destruction the craft had ostensibly been constructed.

"Ostensibly" is perhaps a snide adverb, for it is true that when Benjamin could take time off from the jungle of New York and the killing grounds of the Arctic, he occasionally relaxed by belting his Porsche down the inoffensive Suffolk roads and bombing out into the cold North Sea for a day's slaughter of the big fish. Dressed like a latterday Hemingway at the height of his ambition to prove something, Benjamin was a memorable if not frequent figure to the local fishermen as "Sea Pirate" roared out of the harbour, its skipper's pipe clenched at Popeye tilt between the strong teeth of his jutting jaw, his body at an acute angle to the lofty deck of the flying-bridge as the vessel's aggressive prow lifted to the oncoming waves. Out there, beyond sight of land, strapped into the fighting-chair with a tuna or a shark on his line, Benjamin was as sure of life as his victims were of death.

Sol and Miriam, needless to say, were not in Benjamin's class at all. They were perfectly content with chugging "Sea Pirate" at almost stalling speed across the wide

5

waters inside the low shingle banks that gave protection from the dangers of the North Sea. Even to have read Hemingway would have made Sol tired. Besides, with four gorgeous little girls to entertain, nothing could be more enjoyable and relaxing than to potter down harbour to the sandy bay where the children could swim in perfect safety under their fond grandparents' watchful eyes.

The children loved the water and could swim like fish, never seeming to tire. With the best of summer gone, Jackie had dressed them in the chic little trousers their father had had made for them out of the skins of seal pups culled by his own hands, and these, with sea-blue tops to cover their little brown chests, completed a picture that brought tears to their doting elders' eyes.

"They're so cute," Miriam said, shaking her head, "they're just so cute." She and Sol were sitting side by side at the control panel on the flying-bridge.

"It's warming up," Sol said. "They'll be hot in those trousers."

"Say, I've never seen the tide so far out," Miriam remarked, peering round her through large decorative sunglasses.

"In one hour it will be low water," Sol said. " 'Low water springs', the man at the yard told me."

Miriam nodded. "That means real low." She leaned over the rail and called down to the children who were racing round the main deck with joyful abandon. Two hours of good behaviour in a Rolls Royce is not everyone's idea of a peak experience and there was energy to be expended.

"Now take care," she called. "I don't want any horseplay until we are safely anchored in the bay."

"Don't forget to rub some lotion on Rebecca's back," Sol said. "You know how the sun gets her."

"It's not so strong now," Miriam said. "That's what's so good about September if you pick a real nice day."

But not everything was working out as well as the

6

weather. They were a few hundred yards from the harbour mouth but still half a mile from the bay. Benjamin, had he not been in New York, would have reminded Sol that "Sea Pirate" on a spring tide at an hour before low water could be running into problems.

Something that was a feeling rather than a noise ran through the vessel's fibreglass hull, tickling the palms of Sol's hands where they rested lightly on the steering wheel.

"My God, Miriam," he said, "I think we touched something."

His wife leaned over the rail and peered at the water many feet below.

"I guess you want to be more in the centre," she said. "We're too near the shore, Sol. It curves out just ahead of us."

But the warning came too late. Much more positive contact was made as "Sea Pirate" slid to a gentle but decisive halt, making for herself a comfortable berth in the soft mud that ran up from the harbour bottom to the curving edge of the sand.

"Holy cow," Miriam exclaimed, "we're aground."

Sol had paled a little, for beyond the basic simplicities of starting, steering and stopping "Sea Pirate" he knew less about boats than almost anything else in life. The boatyard maintained the vessel so well that she was always available for instant use, and it had seemed the usual simple matter to potter down to the children's beloved bay. But the day was fine, the breeze gentle, the sky clearing itself of cloud. There was no excuse for negative thinking.

"No cause for panic," he said firmly. "It will be low water in less than an hour. In no time after that we'll float off on the rising tide. I don't think we should even try to reverse off now ; it might damage the propellers." He cut the engines, feeling rather masterful.

Some of his wife's colour returned. "O.K., Sol, I dare

7

say you know best."

Four excited faces appeared on the flying-bridge.

"Granny!" Rebecca said, beaming. "We're ship-wrecked!"

"On a desert island," Paula added, jumping up and down as though on springs.

"For ever and ever," Jacintha confirmed delightedly.

"And ever," supplied Miranda, who was not the most imaginative of the four.

For a moment the children stood quietly in line, expectancy in every feature. There was no movement from "Sea Pirate". They were clearly stuck fast until the tide returned in the afternoon. Sol sold himself the proposition that there was no problem; going aground was all part of the fun.

"All right, you monkeys," he said, "so you wanted to swim. So grandpa's brought you to a good place, huh?"

"Do you think they should?" Miriam said. "The tide may sweep them away."

"Oh, goody," Paula said, "and then we can be wescued." The Rs had always been a problem.

Sol looked over the side. "It will be slack water soon. Until then, play on the sand. But no going in further, mind, than just below your knees. Understand?"

"Understand!" four voices confirmed happily.

"And keep your pants on till it gets warmer," Miriam called. "The wind's still quite chilly." She shivered, crossing her arms over her body. "My God, Sol, there's no-one but us in this whole damned harbour. You realise that?"

"It's mid-week, Miriam. This time in September the trippers have gone. You expect Blackpool?"

They watched the children scamper down the steps from the main deck and into the shallow water in which "Sea Pirate" had beached. At the back of the boat it was still deep, but by the steps it barely covered their ankles. In blissful expectation of a wholly permissive few hours,

8

the children ran shouting on to the drying sands, at once beginning to dig with their hands as though their lives depended on it.

"Hey," Sol called, throwing them buckets and spades, "you forgotten something?"

"It's a nice spot, Sol," Miriam said. "More sand than in the bay."

Sol called out to the children again, cupping his hands. "Come on, now, how about a race to warm you up?"

They were warm already with the overspilling energy of childhood, but the suggestion was agreeable.

"A race, a race," said Rebecca, who was the bossy one. "All line up here." She trailed a ribbon of fine shingle across the white sand.

"To the bigger of those two rocks," Sol shouted, pointing to the far end of the beach where two grey humps lay on the sands between the shingle and the sea.

"On your marks, get set, go!" Miriam commanded, and the children ran in ragged formation along the beach, Rebecca with neat purposive strides, Paula and Jacintha at less than full stretch, and Miranda with her side-flung legs taking up the rear as she always did.

As Rebecca reached the two rocks her grandparents heard her call out, though they were too far away to register the compound of pleasure, astonishment and perhaps a little fear. They saw her bend toward the larger of the rocks, extending her hand and almost touching it, and then she turned round and ran back to the boat, marshalling her sisters to accompany her. Panting with excitement and exertion she called up from the beach:

"Grandpa! Gran! It isn't a rock. You'll never guess. It's a seal. A big one and a baby."

"Oh, don't say that," Miriam exclaimed. "Keep right away, kids. Understand? Don't go near it."

"Why?" Rebecca demanded, still flushed with the pleasure of discovery. "Seals don't bite people. They're lovely."

"They're *lovely*," the others chorused, jumping up and down.

9

Sol shielded his eyes and looked down the beach. The seals had not moved.

"Basking, I suppose," he said. "Well, all right, but don't go too near. Play this end of the beach."

Four faces registered disappointment, but obediently they returned to their digging not far from the boat, though as the minutes went by there was a slight but distinct drift toward the far end of the sands.

"Can we take off our trousers and swim?" Rebecca called when four turrets of sand and an impressive moat were to her credit.

"Not yet," Miriam replied. "The sun's behind that big cloud and the tide's still going out. Soon."

She made coffees and brought the cups to the flying-bridge.

"The kids can have their drinks when they've been in," she said. "They'll like that."

They sat and watched indulgently, sipping their coffees and nibbling Sol's favourite biscuits.

"Those kids have it over any kids ever," Miriam said dotingly.

Sol nodded.

Miriam sat forward suddenly, leaning across the guard rail, narrowing her eyes. "Well, what do you know? There's someone swimming down there."

"That's not a person," Sol said, peering over the rail, "it's another seal."

"For God's sake, so it is," Miriam exclaimed, looking again. "Something to do with the other two, I guess."

"Look, there's another. And another, further out."

As they stared at the still ebbing water they saw more heads appear until they could count at least a dozen, some smaller than others, glistening in the sun that now bathed the sea from an almost cloudless sky. It was like watching a contingent of tanned, moustached colonels taking a quiet remedial dip in some spa.

A big seal, nearest the shore, barked commandingly,

10

and only then did the children look up from their sand-castling and see the visitors. They screamed with delight and raced up and down the sand, waving and calling.

As though finding their pleasure infectious, the seals began to gambol in the water, playfully rushing in all directions, circling, diving and curling above the surface.

"Sol, Sol," Miriam said anxiously. "They might attack the kids."

Sol's face was not free from concern, but he shook his head. "I never heard of a seal attacking anyone," he said, "but all right, maybe we should call them back."

"The two on the beach are leaving," Miriam said. "That's probably what the others were after."

The children were in the surf now, calling out to the seals, finding names for them, deliriously pleased.

"Oh, my God," Miriam said, "they are not going away. They are coming nearer."

It was true. The seals were closer to the shore, sporting and barking, sending up great sheets of spray as they slapped the shallows with flippers and tails. Two of the pups were within feet of the children, who showed no sign of fear.

"Sol!" screamed Miriam. "They're attacking the kids."

She rushed for the steps to the saloon deck, almost losing her balance as she turned to back down them. One of the many large bangles she wore on both arms caught on a stanchion, bruising her flesh. Sol followed, breathless from fear rather than exertion, his face white.

"Get a stick," he called out. "Something to hit them with. Anything."

But by the time they had reached the main deck and armed themselves with winch handles from a locker, the children were a hundred or more yards away, well into the shallows, the grey of their tight little trousers making it difficult to pick them out from the surrounding seals through the cloud of spray.

"Rebecca!" screamed Miriam. "Jacintha! Kids! Come

11

back, come back!" But her voice had no more significance than the cry of a gull above the distant shouts of the joyful little girls and the barking of the cavorting seals.

"Quick!" panted Sol, climbing down on to the wet sand. "For Christ's sake, hurry."

They did their best, but it was soft going in sand still soggy from the receding tide. Higher up, the dry sand's softness was equally impeding. By the time they reached the small flat headland beyond which the children and the seals had retreated, Rebecca, Jacintha, Miranda and Paula were swimming with the seals.

Sol and Miriam stood at the water's edge, agonisingly out of breath, weeping with fear and frustration.

"They'll kill them, Sol, I know they will."

Drawing in huge gulps of air, Sol tried to make calm assessment of the situation. The children were laughing and splashing joyously with the pups while the older seals looked on and swam in attendance like benevolent parents rejoicing in the simple pleasures of the young.

"They're not hurting them, they're playing," Sol said. "We must get near enough to attract their attention."

They stumbled and staggered a few yards further, but then the beach curved back to create a bay, and they could get no closer.

"Oh, God!" Miriam wept. "Oh, God almighty! They are swimming away from us, and the tide is taking them out to sea."

It was as she said. The heads of the seals and the children grew smaller until it was impossible to tell one from the other. The laughter and the barking intermingled and became fainter until nothing could be heard but the dull roar of the waves beyond the harbour's mouth, and nothing could be seen but small dark blobs on the surface of the water, the little heads of children that could be seals, or of seals that might have been children.

# Walking Gertie

" THE TRAGEDY of the British," the Irishman said, "is the terrible poverty of their aspirations."

He raised his glass and drank deeply, his eyes fixed sightlessly on a puddle of beer in the centre of the pub floor.

Harry grunted. At sixty seven he was not planning further self-development. He was enjoying retirement to the hilt, his almost unvarying domestic routine never seeming to stale. His only, if unrealistic, aspiration was the indefinite preservation of habit.

He looked at his watch. "I must be off, then," he said. "Gertie's getting restless."

The bitch wagged her stumpy tail, sensing his mood and finding no quarrel with it. When it came to routine, they were two of a kind. Breakfast, greenhouse, pub, walk, lunch . . . Dog and man co-existed on the even keel of predictable sequence.

Harry rose. "Walkies," he said unnecessarily.

They left The Bear and Honeypot – its name so pointlessly changed, he had felt, from The Earl of Wessex when the trendy Kensington couple took it over – and walked down the village street to the lane that led to the fields. It had to be the shorter walk that day, as a letter had come that needed an answer before the afternoon collection.

Man's brains pack up at three times the speed of women's – or so he had read in The Times that morning – and while he had begun to detect confirming signs in himself (slower reactions, forgetfulness, a greater willingness to let others do the talking – though, all right, some got more garrulous), he sensed that letter writing was a discipline he should not let go. Helen was a devoted wife who was almost certain to outlive him, and she would have been quite willing to take over the paperwork. But their unspoken agreement was that this should be avoided until absolutely necessary. Learning to live with the diminishments of old age had been a mercifully gradual process. Now, with an unindexed but adequate pension, modest savings, a paid-off mortgage, and grandchildren distanced beyond daily contact, but within a reasonable car ride, the years were sliding by serenely enough, imposing little stress except from moments of noting the rapidity of their passing.

True, "Pine Haven" was rather too near the main road for comfort, but that gave an added reason for walking Gertie. A Jack Russell terrier, she stood about ten inches to Harry's five feet six and was marginally his senior – if, that is, you judge a dog's age by the dubious seven-to-one ratio determined by a nation that with notable exceptions tends to pamper its companion animals.

They had got her from the RSPCA shelter a few miles away. An animal liberation group, it was said, had rescued her along with several other dogs and a dazed, sick chimpanzee that had to be put out of its misery, from a research laboratory conducting brain experiments in Crickhurst. Certainly, for a long time any fright or even mild threat brought whimpering and incontinence, followed by days of cringing and quite pitiful distrust. But two years of calm routine and affection at "Pine Haven" appeared to have brought rehabilitation, except that from time to time she lapsed into what in a human might be seen as a day dream, almost a trance. It was as though, Helen remarked, the bitch retreated into another world. But the thought was laughed away almost as soon as she had voiced it.

14

The pattern of their walks never varied except as between clockwise and anti-clockwise, with or without the detour through North Wood. The itinerary was planned to allow Gertie her greatest joy – the proximity of hedgerows. This meant going round rather than across the four fields that were the core of their ritual.

All life went on round the fields' edges; or all life of any interest to Gertie. They were typical Dorset fields, not yet denied by the economics of agribusiness their age-old hedgerows and stretches of dry-stone walling, which in places were hidden by thorn, bramble and old man's beard, and by the countless plants whose sheer weight of numbers ensured their survival from stock and sprays. A refuge for most forms of wild life, their combined scents were a heady challenge to Gertie's perceptive nose. To say that the bitch lived for her walks would be no more of an overstatement than to say that he lived for the pleasure of witnessing her certain joy. It was a simple case of symbiosis. That the rabbits, mice, voles, birds and other creatures of the hedgerows found dog and man's daily routine less congenial is another matter.

Helen was not much of a walker. He was fond of her, of course, but nothing he could have done at this stage of life could have brought her a tenth of the unalloyed pleasure he gave to Gertie by taking her round the fields. Helen's pleasure was responding to their daughter's remarkable number of minor crises needing a grandmaternal presence in Taunton, but she always left Harry with a meal in fridge or larder and was seldom away for a night unless, rarely, very rarely, they went away together. But this hardly ever happened nowadays, as uprooting fussed them both more than it used to, and the doubtful joys of sitting in airports listening to reasons for four, six or eight hour delays had thrown a pall over the alleged delights of going foreign. Never mind the problem of leaving Gertie behind. Abroad, they agreed with Dr Johnson, was worth seeing, but not worth going to see. The fortnightly visit by his daughter, son-in-law and their two boisterous small boys was quite enough to keep him in touch with the "real" world. Rather more than enough, sometimes. If Gertie ever missed a walk it was because two days of the grandchildren prompted "little rests" that invariably led to several hours of unplanned oblivion.

But a life expectation ratio of seven to one – or of a more realistic five to one, for we all know of more "140"-year-old dogs than humans – brings inevitable partings, whether or not accident or age provokes them. In Gertie's case it was the former, bringing a mercifully quick death that broke the nearside front headlamp of a red Ford being driven at three times the speed limit by the skin-headed son of the local vicar, a parson of liberal leanings whose sense of sin was so low-keyed as to make him indistinguishable in dress, deed or word from any of the other regulars of The Bear and Honeypot. His son preferred The Cow and Gate, a five-mile drive away, which proved a pity so far as Gertie was concerned.

For two days Harry did not stir from the house. On the third, Helen, once a nursing sister and with firm views on how to handle life's smaller problems, insisted that they drive to Taunton – "to get you out of yourself." On the fourth she said:

"It's a lovely day. Why not do a little walk?"

"I don't feel much like it. Think I'll watch the football."

"A walk would get you out of yourself."

"You said that yesterday. When we got home I felt no different, only more tired."

"It isn't good for you to brood."

"I couldn't bear to walk round those fields – not without Gertie."

Helen patted his arm. "I do understand, dear, but maybe it is like falling off a bicycle. You know, you should get on again straight away in case you lose the knack."

To please her he put on his walking shoes and took his stick from the hall stand. Helen had remembered to remove Gertie's lead from its hook near the door, putting it out of sight in the broom cupboard.

He stood on the curb, waiting for two cars and a trio of young people on mountain bikes to allow him to cross. He muttered "Come on, Gertie" under his breath, then crossed the road, wanting her company so much that he could almost see her dashing ahead of him.

He walked the field joylessly, stopping by some of the gaps and burrows which Gertie had explored with maximum enthusiasm He ached to see her, head on one side, the pointed intelligent face, ears cocked, emerging from the familiar breaks in the hedges and walls. But the fields were empty, not merely of Gertie, but seemingly of most other life, now undisturbed by the bitch's regular scouring of the fields' perimeters. He returned home, and over a glass of sherry before lunch shed a few tears which shamed him by their self-pity.

Helen persisting, he walked the fields most days from then on, but the ache and the expectation did not lessen. He went on responding to all the minor excitements that had stimulated Gertie to frantic dashes and barking – the flashing scut of a rabbit diving into its burrow, the clatter of pigeons' wings, the sudden rise of an alarmed pheasant or grouse – and each response was followed by the flattening realisation that it was not being shared.

One day in early autumn he was sheltering under a tree from a sudden shower. Fifty yards further on a pair of rabbits was feeding peacefully, unaware of his presence. He had not moved or made any noise, and was to leeward of the rabbits, but suddenly they jumped in opposite directions, as though something had come upon them without warning. One rabbit darted into the hedge, but the other ran further into the open field and sat on its haunches, its body tense with fear. A youngster, he supposed, too green to make for the nearest cover. He looked into the sky to see if a hawk had alarmed them, but detected no such reason. Surprised by their behaviour, he

17

moved along the hedgerow to see what could have accounted for the frantic impulse to flee, and this made the rabbit shoot off again, this time in his direction, but zigzagging as though escaping the jaws of some predator. It saw him, swerved, and dived into the hedge some ten yards away.

When he got home he told Helen about the rabbits' behaviour, but she was not a countrywoman and could offer no sensible explanation.

"Hares do funny things, don't they?" she said. "Maybe it was a young hare."

"I can tell a rabbit from a hare," he replied stiffly. "It must have been a hawk I just didn't notice."

That year two of the fields had been sown to barley, and on one warm morning he stopped to rest on a bank above the larger of the fields. He had often done so with Gertie who liked nothing more than to indulge in real or imaginary pursuit through the standing corn. She had never, to his knowledge, caught anything, except once when a pheasant, aware of the dangers of taking to the air in retreat from man, had run into some wire netting and been trapped, getting away with its life for the loss of a mouthful of feathers.

It was one of those still autumn days that suggest, however deceptively, that the world is at peace beneath a benevolent sun and that time, on poetical licence, has opted to stand still. Harry, his back supported by a fencing post, pulled his hat brim over his eyes, the better to look out over the golden carpet, and began to pull the beard off an ear of barley picked from the path around the field. There had been little wind for some weeks and the barley was standing strong and straight, as though asking for harvest.

He noticed a disturbance in the corn, about a third of the way into the field. Just a ripple in the barley heads, such as he had watched many a time before when Gertie had picked up the scent of some sheltering creature. He

18

wondered idly whether a hare or bird was making the ripple, but it was too steady and purposive. A fox, perhaps. The ripple moved one way and then another, and then it seemed to accelerate and was heading in an almost straight line toward the bank. He leaned forward, now intent and curious, hoping that whatever it was would emerge and reveal its identity. He wished he had a camera, for the edge of the field was no more than four metres away, and whatever was running through the corn must become visible as it emerged into the thinner, shorter fringe of barley alongside the path.

As the heads of corn were parting a mere two metres from the edge of the field, Harry held his breath, careful to make no movement or noise that might cheat him of an identification. The ripple came straight to him, all the way to the field's edge, moving even a few stalks in the thinner fringe. But no bird or animal obliged him with the opportunity to identify it. Bewildered, he looked out over the corn again to see if by any chance the creature had spotted him and had run back into cover, betraying its retreat by renewed ripples. But the whole area of corn was still and silent beneath the hot sun.

Helen was a practical woman and gave no more credence to this story than to his report of the startled rabbit.

"The wind plays funny tricks," she reminded him. "Think of those extraordinary circles they thought had been made by UFOs."

"Wind my foot," he said. "I know the sign of an animal moving through corn."

"Neither of us has the eyesight we enjoyed at twenty."

He grunted. "Nor the naive belief that the other person isn't necessarily a blithering idiot."

Other equally puzzling things occurred during subsequent walks. A stoat that appeared to be standing at bay against some unseen threat; the pawmarks of a dog alongside his own footprints in the lane leading to the fields, noticed only when he returned from his walk in January snow; the ginger cat who crossed his path and suddenly arched into a bristling hoop of hissing threat, staring fixedly not at him but at empty air two feet from his right boot.

If inexplicable to him, these small experiences were not a source of doubt or surprise to Helen. But she was not an unkind woman and curbed her instinct for deflation. Later she was glad that she had done so. It had been a hard winter, and after the incident of the pawmarks in the snow, Harry declined suddenly. Early in April, when the winds were still cold and the daffodils beginning to dip their crumpled heads, without warning Helen became a widow.

They had gone to bed, and Harry as usual was reading before turning out the light. Helen, a sound sleeper, took no more than three minutes to reach deep sleep night in and night out, somewhat to Harry's annoyance when he had had a particularly poor night and she awoke to chide him for taking another half hour; sound sleepers seldom shed sympathy at tales of others' wakefulness.

On this, their last evening, Harry had gone to the spare bedroom across the landing to find a back number of the DIY magazine he was reading, leaving Helen already asleep. He found the magazine and must have sat on the guests' double bed; for when Helen came across him there in the morning he was lying on his back on the duvet, his legs half off the bed, the magazine on the floor near his right foot.

It was a good enough way to go, and if the doctor's later diagnosis was to be believed, probably instantaneous. Indeed, he looked so peaceful, so natural, that Helen, ever the servant of commonsense, stood for a few moments at the foot of the bed, quite devoid of tears at that early stage of bereavement, regarding her husband with a strange mix of feeling. On the one hand she was sure that he must be dead; on the other, she was thankful at how happy and resigned he looked, almost as though his departure had been the result of tidy planning.

What was unusual, even curious, possibly (dare it be said?) inexplicable about Harry's passing was not the event itself, which was only to be expected of a man who had experienced the span that most of us believe is our due, but the state of the clean pink duvet which Helen had herself plumped up only the previous morning.

For near the end of the bed, within inches of Harry's legs, was a hollow, a compression, or – if you like – the unmistakable indentation made by any dog in any duvet on which he or she had been able to get away with a good night's sleep.

Just as strange, on the floor at the foot of the bed, below the indentation, lay Gertie's lead. If Helen had forgotten hiding it at the back of the broom cupboard, Harry for sure had never known that it had been put there. Washing up and the garden were the extent of his domestic commitments.

On and off in the months and years to come, Helen thought about this odd incident and tried to find a rational explanation. But the problem usually came into her mind just before she went to sleep in her solitary bed, and being one of these people blessed with the knack of inviting rapid oblivion she never got the chance to come to any very satisfactory conclusion. Which is probably as well, because it would almost certainly not have been the correct one.

# A Little Of What You Fancy

" I WANT TO eat you," she said.

"Mmmmmmmmmm?"

He had been fast asleep.

"I want to eat you."

"No' now, darlin'. Shleepy."

He turned his back on her, his eyes still closed, and wriggled into new comfort.

She shook him by the shoulder.

"Paul! Do you hear me? I want to *eat* you."

His mind struggled through layers of sleep to grapple with her words. His arm fumbled for his watch.

"It's four in the morning, darling. You don't usually get sexy-poo at four in the morning."

"Sexy-poo" was unfortunate, but it had stuck.

"I'm not feeling sexy," she said. "I'm trying to tell you. I want to eat you. Can't you recognise a cry for help?"

He pushed himself into a sitting position and ran his hands over his eyes and hair.

"Oh, come on, sweetie, I've a hell of a day ahead."

"Paul, listen, you've got to believe me. I mean just what I say. I have this awful urge to eat you."

"*Eat* me?"

"Eat you. Literally."

"You mean, eat my flesh?"

"Yes. Just now I nearly bit into your side where your pyjamas weren't quite meeting. Your spare tyre seemed irresistibly succulent."

"I haven't got a . . . " He was more or less awake now. "You honestly mean to tell me that you want to eat my flesh?"

"Yes, yes, yes. I keep on telling you."

"Raw?"

"Raw."

"Just as it is?"

"Just as it is. No sauces, no spices, not even salt."

"Good God! Are you feeling all right?"

"Well of course I'm not feeling all right if I want to eat my husband."

"In yourself, I mean."

"I haven't a temperature or a pain or anything. Just this tremendous urge for raw, juicy flesh."

"My raw, juicy flesh."

"Yes."

"Not anyone else's?"

"I don't know that anyone else's would have the same appeal. I hope not."

"I don't know. It might be a good idea to spread it around a bit." He was still short on belief.

"If you feel this is a time for quips . . . "

"Sorry. It's just so . . . Have you felt this way before?"

"A little bit. Yesterday when I woke up. I assumed I needed breakfast."

"You had extra rashers."

"And your sausage. It doesn't seem to have helped."

"But the feeling passed off?"

"At the time. I felt rather thirsty through the day, though."

"You must be missing something. You'd better see Rutherford first thing."

Doctor Rutherford was puzzled.

"I've never met this one before," he admitted.

"Nor have I," Fenella said. "I hope I'm not making medical history." It was not facetiousness. She knew trailblazers took all the first-time risks.

"Do you feel the urge to eat *me*?" Rutherford asked.

"Not at the moment," Fenella said. "But then I can't smell your flesh across this desk. It's different when you are in bed with someone. When they are warm and close and have that subtle perfume of a joint just taken out of the oven." The memory brought a touch of moisture to her pretty lips.

"Quite so," Rutherford murmured, tipping his chair towards the window.

"So what am I going to do about it?" Fenella said. She was a woman who liked people to get to the point.

"You're not a vegetarian, are you?" the doctor enquired.

"Certainly not."

"You have a normal diet?"

"Very normal."

"Balanced?"

"I'd say so." They always read the "Living" pages in the Sundays.

"Meat's a terrible price these days. Tempting to cut down. Some people eat those analogue things."

"We haven't cut down."

"Does this urge go away when you have just eaten meat?"

"I haven't felt it during the day. Only the last two nights in bed."

Doctor Rutherford looked up at the ceiling, pressed his finger tips together, filled his ample cheeks with air, and puffed at a meandering fly.

"It is too soon for me to make a confident diagnosis. I think you should come back in a week's time. There's possibly some slight glandular imbalance."

"Paul thinks I am turning into a cannibal. 'Slight glandular imbalance' is rather an under-statement."

"I can understand his concern. But we must not get things out of perspective. The body's chemistry can play

24

strange tricks."

"But what if I start to tear at Paul's throat during the night? I could kill him."

"It isn't that uncontrollable, is it?"

"It was a near thing last night."

"If it overcame you, could you not aim at a less vulnerable point? The forearm, for instance?"

"I don't think Paul wants to lose any of his forearm. He's a keen gardener."

"It shouldn't go that far. The first nip will wake him. Keep a pillow between you for a few nights."

"Well, I'll try," Fenella said.


"Well, that's marvellous!" Paul said. "Bloody marvellous! The recipe for a sound night's sleep."

"He's baffled."

"There must be something he can do. Even if only a muzzle."

"He thinks the body chemistry must have gone a bit wrong. Perhaps it will adjust itself. Nature's a wonderful thing."

"It can't be the menopause. You're too young."

"And I'm not pregnant, pubescent, adolescent or senile. None of the stock excuses."

"You're probably short of protein. Some people need more than others. We'll go to the Steak House tonight. A steak rarer than your usual will put you on your feet."


"Ow! Oo! Christ Almighty!"

Paul shot up in bed, his right hand clamped to his left shoulder.

"Whadyerwannadothatfor?" he demanded, his voice thick with sleep and pain. Then he remembered. "Oh, God!" he said.

He pulled the light cord.

Fenella pushed herself up on to the pillows, her eyes still heavy with sleep.

"Was I . . . ?" she began.

"Look what you've done!" Paul demanded. He took his hand from his shoulder to reveal teeth marks and a few specks of blood.

"Oh, darling," Fenella said, appalled. Her tongue stroked her lips. "Here, let me lick it for you."

He jerked away from her.

"Keep off!" he said. "You're a vampire."

"Paul! I'm your wife. Do you think I *meant* to bite you?"

"It was a jolly good imitation of intent."

"I was half asleep."

"The other half had teeth."

"I'll bathe it."

"What the hell are we going to do?" Paul said. "We can't go on like this."

"The smell of this disinfectant sort of turns me off. Perhaps if I dabbed it on your arms and chest tonight . . . "

"Brilliant! What a rôle! Bad smell or quick snack."

"And keep your jacket done up at the neck. I know it's warm, but the less I smell you the better."

"Here! Steady! Ouch! Oh, God! Leggo!"

But Fenella's dainty, slightly receding teeth were sunk deeply, agonisingly into his left hip. She was making quick snuffly sounds, half growl, half contentment, like a puppy at its bowl.

He slapped her head and grabbed her neck, writhing away from her. She let go of him and pulled back, her expression dazed, blood on her lower lip, her eyes blinking as the light went on.

"But I want . . . " she began, then tuned into the situation; but her eyes returned to his bleeding hip and there was a hint of hunger in them.

"For God's sake!" Paul shouted. "You're bloody mad!"

The violence of his protest bludgeoned her brain into normality.

"I'm not, darling, I'm not. I just couldn't resist . . . I

26

wasn't really awake . . . It wasn't you I was eating . . . "

"It bloody was me."

"I mean, I didn't think of it being you. It was some sort of blind instinct."

She bathed his wound tenderly.

"Do you think I'd better have a tetanus jab?" he said.

"It might be wise."

"That long canine of yours has gone really deep."

"Go to Rutherford on the way to work."

"I don't feel much like work, thank you very much. God knows what you'll do if you're left alone. The postman, the milkman . . . "

"Even so," she said, "it might be better if we aren't together more than we need while this thing works itself out."

"You don't think she might be rabid?" Paul asked.

Doctor Rutherford smiled tolerantly.

"Highly unlikely, I'd say. It really is a most extraordinary case."

"Fascinating to the whole medical fraternity, no doubt, but what's the next step? God knows what bit of me she'll have a go at next."

"I think a sedative is indicated. Make sure she takes it."

"You bet I will," Paul said fervently.

They both slept late, Fenella because of the sedative, Paul because of two disturbed and traumatic nights.

When he woke it was daylight and Fenella was chewing gently at his hand, her eyes closed and her breathing that of someone more asleep than awake.

He got up and made some strong coffee for them both. When he returned Fenella was spread out over the bed, half on her side, one arm above her head, her thin nightie clinging to her slim figure as though arranged by a girlie mag. photographer. Paul told himself how beautiful she was, but there was something inside him that was even

27

stronger than the urge to take her in his arms.

They lay side by side, drinking their coffees.

"So the sedative worked," Fenella said, relief in her voice.

"Not quite," Paul said. "You were doing your best to bite my hand off, but you were too doped to make a good job of it."

Fenella put her cup down and buried her face in her hands.

"Oh, no!"

Paul grimaced. "It's not much of a prospect. Limited consumption under permanent sedation. There must be someone else we can go and see."

"Addiction," the dietician said. "That's my view. I had a patient once who was crazy about bananas. Couldn't get enough of them. Bananas over bananas, you might say."

"But why Fenella? We eat a perfectly normal diet – a bit high in protein from what you say, but normal enough by Western standards."

The other shrugged.

"Who can say? We have come so far from the dietary patterns for which our physiology is suited. We are only beginning to understand these things."

"Charming! So I might as well expose my throat and let her get on with it."

"You say your wife is partial to underdone meat. My guess is that she has reached a point beyond which she can only be satisfied by raw flesh in excess."

"Won't it be enough if she just eats butcher's meat uncooked?"

"Unwise for several reasons, especially if her craving is on a par with that of an alcoholic for alcohol."

"Oh, God! Meat-eaters' Anonymous?"

"Look," the dietician said, laying a friendly hand on Paul's shoulder, "try not to worry about it. There are more things in heaven and earth . . . you know the

28

quotation. Show a lot of understanding and give your wife plenty of salads. As fresh as possible."

"She's never been very keen on salads and fruit."

"That may be a pointer."

"The children and I eat most of the stuff I grow."

"Increase your output. Buy a good recipe book. Do your best to tempt her."

"My cos lettuce have been good this year," Paul said. "Got them started early. The beans are promising, too. Nearly everything's doing well."

The dietician nodded. "Rutherford was telling me. You are quite a self-sufficiency buff."

"Well, we grow all we can. Pigs, chickens, guinea fowl, quail. Nothing like your own birds, you know. We get through a tremendous number."

"Fine, fine! But just for the time being I'd like you to cut out the meat for your wife. Cheese, all right. Nuts if she likes them. Rice, beans, all that kind of thing. They contain all the protein we need. Go to a health food stores. They'll have ideas."

"Bloody hell!" Paul said. "She's not going to enjoy that."

"You never know. It's surprising what people can take to."

Fenella was not keen on the new regime to start with, but by the end of the first week she had almost stopped complaining. By the third she admitted to feeling extraordinarily well.

"I've not thought about meat for days," she said.

"Does meat include me?"

"Yes, darling, you too."

"But we haven't been within two feet of each other for ages. Not for *any* purpose."

"Poor pet," Fenella said, patting his hair at arm's length, "it's not for want of desire, believe me. It just seemed sensible."

Paul rubbed his hip. "I see that," he said.

"Give it another week," Fenella urged, "and then . . . "

"That," Paul said, turning off the light, "was proof that absence really does do the trick."

"More than one trick," Fenella said thankfully. "We must send that dietician man a sack of nuts at Christmas."

"I'd rather give him a bird. We're not getting through them without you."

Fenella pulled a face. "I never thought I'd take to raw foods so readily."

"If they had anything to do with the past half-hour," Paul said, "you could be on to a good thing."

"You don't know what you're missing," Fenella said sleepily. "Everything seems to taste so much better now. Sometimes I dream about baskets of fruit and vegetables. Good night, sexy-poo."

"Night – Tiger."

Weeks passed. Fenella did not revert so much as to nibble her husband's ear except in a non-gastronomical context. One day Paul suggested she try a little meat again, offering to kill and cook the plumpest hen in the run.

"I'll use that recipe with brandy and oranges," he tempted.

Fenella declined with a vehemence that was almost disgust. There seemed no point in arguing. Nor did he really want to. Since he and the children had begun to make things easier for Fenella by sharing her diet on most days, the housekeeping budget had shown a healthy surplus. The cost of feeding the now almost stable fowl population was rather a drain, but Paul had thinned their ranks by giving some away.

Summer merged into early autumn, but September improved upon July. It had been an excellent season in the garden, and the apple and plum trees were heavy with fruit.

On a warm night in the last week of the month Paul woke soon after dawn to find that he was alone in bed. He lay on his back and gazed at the ceiling, expecting Fenella to return from the bathroom.

She did not do so. He called her name. He wondered if she was capping a poor night with a cup of tea, so put on his slippers and went downstairs. The house was quiet, the kitchen empty. But the back door was ajar, which was not how he had left it after putting out the cat. Puzzled, he closed the door, then opened it, remembering that the dog next door had once prompted Fenella to rescue a cornered, protesting Tinkles.

He walked out on to the concrete path bordering the extensive kitchen garden, and there he saw Fenella. She was kneeling on the bare soil in her thin nightie, looking like a huge white rabbit with hanging golden hair. She was eating a lettuce, ravenously, and her other hand held a radish and a spring onion. Around her, the carefully tended saladings that had made the dietician's advice so easy to follow might have been invaded by a flock of sheep. The ground was churned up and the broken stems of several lettuce plants were still weeping their milky sap.

In the background, on a high mound of compost, splendid against the risen sun, stood their great brown rooster, sire of a hundred consumed cockerels. Paul looked at the rooster, and the rooster looked at Paul, then stretching his powerful neck he gave vent to a prolonged crow that rattled a loosened pane in the window above the kitchen sink. There was challenge, even a note of triumph, in it.

Paul gazed at the scene for a few moments, then went back into the kitchen, feeling in need of time in which to think of something to do or say that would be remotely contributory.

Outside, Fenella was attacking a carrot as though she had never before met an edible root.

31

# Bishop's Move

THE BRITISH take pride in being reserved. I have long suspected that "reserve" is an agreeable euphemism for the simple fact that behind that phlegmatic exterior very little is going on. But I could be wrong. I was about Frank.

Everyone always said that Frank would end up a bishop, and he for one never denied the possibility. Indeed, he actively worked at it. Which meant, of course, that he was a very political animal, for you do not rise through the clerical ranks without knowing what makes the temporal world tick. Politics and idealism are uneasy bedfellows. Jesus Christ would not have made it as a sidesman.

But it was not until we discovered a mutual liking for chess that I knew Frank other than to exchange High Street pleasantries about cricket and the weather. The boredom and predictability of his sermons had long before convinced me that I was an Easter-and-Christmas-only churchgoer. His congregation in that charming if not exactly radical part of West Sussex was small but faithful, mostly gentleman farmers, retired army and navy, and local gentry. Reserve and containment were what they understood. They knew exactly what to expect of Frank, and they got it every time. For anyone wanting to study the Tory party at prayer, St Mark in the Meadow, East Burpham, was tops.

What eventually happened would have astonished me even more had our weekly chess encounters not brought a degree of intimacy he shared with no-one else. With no-one else, that is, but Angela Elfin-Davis, the beautiful doe-eyed, dark-haired daughter of a widely respected and well connected Welsh minister. She moved into Frank's life and heart a year or two before he made the grade of archdeacon, and he was besotted by her.

"Watch that young man," my wife remarked shortly before she died, "he's going places. That girl knows what she's about."

Sure enough, not all that long after the marriage, Frank's archdeaconry was confirmed, and although to his female parishioners' disappointment the ensuing years did not bless their union with issue, their devotion to each other seemed not one jot diminished.

On an April day of uncertain weather, Frank and I were setting up our pieces for a new game.

"There are whispers," I said, "about a suffragan being appointed before long. I'm white this time, I think."

Frank nodded. "I shall be sorry to leave this parish."

"It's that certain, then?"

"Consecration should be announced any day."

"Congratulations. When do you bang on the door?"

"Bang?"

"Don't new bishops bang on the door on consecration day?"

He had the build of a full back and the features of a film idol; it was charm and application rather than quickness of mind that had helped him up the ladder.

"Oh, I see. Just after Christmas, I think."

"Angela must be pleased. You'll be an unusually youthful bishop."

"Yes," he said, "I suppose she will be pleased."

"You sound doubtful."

"I think she would have liked to return to Wales. The hills call to her, she says."

"She'll acclimatize."

"Maybe. I'm just hoping there won't be too many life-

33

style problems."

"Life . . . ? Ah!" I said, "you mean the . . . " I waved a hand " . . . meat and drink business."

It was no secret that Angela, some years Frank's junior, was a teetotaller by family tradition, and until marriage an active campaigner for animals' rights. Rumour had it that pre-marriage she had carried many a banner in Bristol and points west. That wasn't quite Frank's style, and his concession to teetotalism was less than total; but in the matter of walnuts and two vegs he was wholly committed. It had been a sudden conversion to what he called a harmless diet. Until he met Angela he was a perfectly normal flesh-pots man.

"You know how it is with most bishops," he said.

I nodded. "And old Crumpton is no exception."

"We had him to dinner recently, and quite frankly it got a bit sticky."

"You don't mean you offered him Ribena?"

"Lord, no, he got his wine. Angela had grape juice and he never knew. But she drew the line at giving him meat, so she did a nut roast."

I whistled. "Old Crumpton tucking into a mock duck strains the imagination a little."

"It wasn't *shaped* like a duck," Frank said defensively. "Angela wouldn't go that far. It was just a perfectly honest nut roast."

"And delicious they can be," I said stoutly. "I remember the one you gave me very well. The chestnuts and pineapple slices round the edge were particularly good."

"It wasn't the roast itself so much as the ensuing theology that was a trifle worrying," Frank said, countering my knight to king's bishop three with queen to rook five.

I took his pawn. "A bit of bible bashing over the coffee, you mean?"

He grimaced. "That kind of thing."

"I know animals' rights are all the rage," I said, "but

churchmen have never had much to say about non-humans' place in the scheme of things."

He rose and paced the carpet.

"Quite. And, frankly, these last couple of years with Angela have opened my eyes a bit. Her angle is that we can hardly expect better treatment from each other until we stop exploiting the weaker species. It makes such absolute sense."

"You're in love," I said. "It always makes things seem clearer. Some things, anyway."

"You probably won't believe it," he said, "but for a year or more now there have been times when I have looked at my congregation and wondered if I was right to let them off the hook a moment longer."

"I'm not sure I'm with you," I said. "I daresay you'll be wanting to take my pawn next."

"Very well." He stopped and made his move before continuing his pacing. "What I mean is, I get sudden urges to let 'em have it good and strong."

"Good Lord!" I said. "I'd never have thought it."

"If you turned up more often, you might have noticed signs of tension."

"I was there the other day. You seemed pretty . . . normal."

"Well, I can tell you, I get very churned up inside at times."

"Anyway," I said, "I take it you haven't actually . . . let them have it?"

He had forgotten about the chess. He stopped his pacing and began to warm his bottom at the log fire. May still seemed a long way off, yet it was a clammy day with a threat of thunder in the air. I moved my bishop to knight three without any real hope of a response, though pawn to rook five was strongly indicated.

"Just wait until the New Year," he said.

"Why the New Year?"

"I'll be a bishop by then."

"And able to let your hair down?"

35

"Why not? I'll be as far up the tree as I'm likely or really want to get."

"I can't think of many archbishops with dietetic hang-ups, I grant you. Pig farming and good cellars seem more their line."

"It's not only that. Angela is very wrapped up in the Glastonbury Circle."

This was new to me.

"Sounds rather druidical, if that's the word."

"It's more on psychic lines. I can't say I go along with it myself."

"It'd be pushing the boat out a bit far," I admitted. "Psychic, you say. You mean, spiritualism? There *is* a certain mysterious other-worldliness about her."

"Not spiritualism exactly. More a belief in malign and benign influences; predestination; occult pressures."

"Doesn't sound terribly Crumpton," I agreed.

"I feel I'm chancing my arm enough as it is without getting into that kind of thing."

"You're not feeling cooler about the animals' rights issue?"

"Definitely not. I'd go to the stake over that. Angela is the most tender-hearted and lovely girl in the world and I have not had a moment's doubt for years. It was just a bit of a struggle at the beginning when I smelled bacon."

"I'd keep a low profile over the occult business, though."

"I intend to."

The storm had crept up with little warning. There was a tremendous clap of thunder simultaneously with a flash of lightning that filled the room. In the silence that followed, the fire crackled and spat, seemingly before the downpour to come, but perhaps due to an advance rain-drop down the wide straight chimney.

"That was a big one," I said. "Well, it's your move." He left the fire and sat down again.

"I say," he said, "look at that."

36

I leaned forward. Immediately above the board I could smell the very faintest trace of burning. On my king's rook five square was a small scorched imprint of a crucifix, less than an inch long.

"It must have been an ember," I said.

"But where is it? The ember?"

"Burned itself out, I suppose."

"Odd."

"Very odd. Your move, then."

Except for Remembrance Sunday I didn't go to church again until Christmas, but I continued to play chess with Frank and had no reason to suppose from his conversation and bearing, or from local rumour, that he had done anything to blot his copybook before the congregation of St Mark in the Meadow.

His consecration had been duly announced in the spring. He didn't mention the subject when we played chess, but I knew from friends in the village that his and Angela's dinner invitations had been more frequent since news of his appointment. I wondered, idly, how they were making out over the meat question, but it wasn't until our last game before Christmas that the subject came up.

"We've been using this TVP stuff," he said.

"TVP? Sounds like an antiseptic."

"Textured vegetable proteins. Meat analogues."

"Imitation meat?"

I had heard of the stuff. My older girl had gone through a West Country commune phase before settling for her barrister in Parsons Green.

"You can do a lot with it. Almost anything, in fact, that you do with the real thing. But curries and chilli con carne are the best. Indistinguishable."

"Well, yes," I said, "you get this ethnic kind of food wherever you go these days. Even the Chetwynde-Stroodes were dishing out great dollops of rather murky rice the other day. Because it's cheaper, I suppose. But what about

Christmas? Don't tell me they do convincing TVP turkeys."

"We'll be having Christmas at home, so the problem won't arise."

I smiled. "You'll get by until you make the bishopric, then, and after that you can stop pussy-footing?"

"You make me sound rather calculating."

I shrugged. "I'm not judging. It's a rough world and we all have to look ahead a bit to survive."

"I'm getting some stick from Angela."

"Because you're ambitious?"

"She doesn't seem to grasp, bless her, that spiritual ambition hinges on the logistics of the material variety. No rank, no power."

"A good old army truism," I agreed.

"And she's more into this Glastonbury thing than ever. She damned . . . very nearly brought it up when we had Portsmouth and Winchester to dinner recently."

"My God!" I said. "And on top of almond rissoles and grapefruit juice!"

He didn't see it as a subject for levity.

"She's a dear, wonderful, marvellous girl, and her whole attitude to non-human species is totally commendable, but I will confess that when she carries on about malign influences I get a little warm under the collar."

"Never mind," I said, "it is very good for a bishop's wife to have *some* sense of good and evil. I think that's check."

I should have got to the church earlier. It was bitterly cold and I had supposed the turnout would not be large. I couldn't have been more wrong. What with the season and the fact that it would be Frank's last sermon before going on to higher things, the place was packed. I had to be content with a pew too near the door for comfort but with a good side-on view of most of the congregation. Frank was almost invisible behind a Saxon pillar.

I saw almost all the locals and several craggy faces that

38

were unfamiliar. One of these was sitting next to old Crumpton, and they seemed to be exchanging notes. I could guess why they were there and that Frank must be feeling nervous.

But his voice rang strong and confident, and when he began his sermon I could tell it was going to be business as usual. Maybe it was my rapidly freezing feet, but his deep drone seemed slower and more episcopal than ever, and his sermon was so packed with platitudes and undemanding exhortations that the forthcoming ceremony of consecration struck me as a quite unnecessary endorsement of the obvious. To all intents and purposes Frank was a fully fledged bishop of the old school, totally in control of his congregation, expecting nothing of them but their presence and fiscal contribution, a predictable link with all they needed or wanted to know of a higher power.

Half suspecting incipient hypothermia, for my legs were dead to the groin, I was beginning to doze off when there was a deafening noise and a blinding flash which it took some moments to recognise as the arrival of a thunder storm. It was followed by an absolute silence, doubtless because the congregation were half stunned by an explosion that could have been in the church itself. Even Frank stopped speaking, and no doubt his ear drums were ringing as loudly as mine. Then, as his audience began to shuffle and whisper, some rattling their fingers in their ears to restore normal hearing, he resumed his address. But now his voice was louder, more urgent, less slow.

"Oh, but why," he demanded, his tone challenging and almost derisive, "why do I stand before you in the role of suppliant, asking your respect for virtues you have no desire or intention to observe; exhorting you to obey rules that you consciously and determinedly break every day of your life; pleading that you show a compassion and a sense of kinship totally foreign to your coarsened and unrepentant natures? Why do we not admit that the devil's time has come? That all of you here – yes, every man, woman and child – have long since sold your souls to the powers of evil, for all that you have sanctified your thoughtless actions by loyalty to habit and tradition. Christmas! The season of good cheer and goodwill. The time we remember gentle Jesus meek and mild and are full only of loving kindness toward our relatives and neighbours. Rubbish and balderdash! Christmas! The time of gluttony and calculated giving. Of booze, plethora and boredom. Of mindless idleness or cruel, pointless blood-sports over the cold fields, the values of Jesus as far removed from your all too human and self-centred minds as the fate of those harmless birds and beasts whose bodies are even now sizzling in your time-controlled ovens. Shall I tell you who should be sitting in your pews? All the weak and timid creatures who, at your tables and for your shallow pleasures, you have eaten, beaten, chased and tortured in the three hundred and sixty five sanguinary days since we last celebrated this gruesome moment in the year's calendar. I wish I could restore each and every one of them to life and assure them that the kingdom of God has indeed come and that henceforth they need never again fear the cruel hearts and hands of *Homo sapiens*, the creator of pain and suffering, the greatest bully this unhappy world has ever known."

He drew breath.

"But the birds and beasts are not before me, are they? No, only row upon row of pop-eyed human faces, all in a state of hypnotic fascination at the sight of an archdeacon who has obviously gone clean off his rocker. And you will return home, all of you: Colonel Barker and his lady, both as resolute in the hunting field as in their brain-washing of gullible young men recruited to slaughter our politicians' chosen enemies; Sir Rupert Redpill of drug company fame, and Mr Peter Facecoat the cosmetic tycoon, in whose laboratories countless defenceless animals have been tortured over the past year to make another brand-

40

name acceptable to a public already surfeited in alternatives; Mr Mark Slittingham, our distinguished farmer and landowner, whose battered pigs and chickens have brought ugly, stinking Belsens with full planning approval to so many green fields, and whose pursuit of wider recognition has prompted him to give serious money to scientists hell-bent on implanting human genes into other species so that before long Mr Slittingham may be indistinguishable from his best boar ... "

I rose quietly and left. It was all too painful. I walked slowly home through the empty village to my cottage and put fresh logs on the smouldering fire. I looked gloomily at the chess table, remembering our many games. It is so difficult to find agreeable company of precisely one's own standard.

Frank and Angela's Christmas card had fallen from the mantelpiece and was lying in the hearth. I picked it up and put it with the others. As I did so I noticed that the card bore a scorch mark, strangely enough in the form of a cross – not a crucifix, but the ordinary kind that doubles so oddly for the kiss of love or death – and it had just about obliterated Frank's name. Presumably the card had fallen on some hot ash.

Presumably.

# Someone's Birthday

Well-appointed is how the agents would have described the house, had the Hammonds been selling. But the Hammonds were not selling. They were very attached to "Marbella" which purred with fresh paint, double-glazing, eight-inch roof insulation, luxury kitchen, two Hollywood bathrooms, and every other comfort imaginable to an owner who was in the building trade anyway.

The colours, perhaps, were not to everyone's taste, nor the surfeit of wrought iron, the liberal statuary, the crinkle-edged fishpond, and the fulsomely upholstered leisure furniture that was brought out (plastic-wrapped on days of threatening showers) from May to September. But *chacun*, as the French so democratically say, *à son goût*.

The car rolled down the pristine tarmac drive into the quiet estate road. Like the house, it bore evidence of a keen eye for those minor status symbols that keep the neighbours informed of the pecking order.

Malcolm Hammond pulled into the curb and went back to close the intricately designed gates.

"Paid the milkman?" he asked, fitting his seatbelt.

"In the envelope, with the note cancelling."

"You didn't say for how long?"

"I'm not a fool, you know. Just 'until further notice'."

He looked in his wing mirror and pulled away from the curb.

"I should have put a second lock on the side door. I asked you to remind me."

She chain-lit a fresh cigarette. "No-one's been burgled round us in months." Like most women, she could be philosophical on the brink of a holiday. Even the best-appointed kitchens can pall.

He sighed the sigh of a man over-burdened.

"Well, if the bastards mean to get in they'll take a jemmy to the frames, so there's no mileage in worrying."

"That's right," Angie said, settling back comfortably in the glistening purple nylon upholstery. She looked at her gold watch whose 18 carat strap was rather too cushioned by her plump wrist. "Mother and the children should be there by now."

Malcolm grunted. "I hope she airs our beds."

"Handy, having the caravan in her garden."

The car stopped at the lights. The wind had got up and was tearing at the plastic sheeting wrapped round the contents of the roof rack.

"Did you remember the gumboots?" he asked, half turning toward the back seat which was almost filled by the golden labrador.

"And the anoraks," she confirmed. "In the boot."

"Come *on*," he said to the traffic lights.

They turned left, then right and on to the new road that led to the motorway.

"Where are you going to do it?" she asked.

"A few miles along," he said.

"Near the town?"

"Not far."

"I don't know what the children are going to say."

"By the time we're back they'll almost have forgotten. Three weeks're a long time for kids."

"I doubt Sandra'll accept it that easily. She's daft about animals."

"She'll have to, won't she?"

"Even so . . . "

His grip on the wheel tightened. "It's better this way. We agreed."

43

She shrugged. "Suppose so."

They were on the motorway and he put the car up to eighty in the centre lane. It was at the top end of the Ford range and there was still plenty of give in the pedal.

"When we've had the week with the kids," he said, "it'll be nice to get her abroad. Blow the dust out of her."

"It hasn't had its first full service yet," Angie said. "There can't be much 'dust' in it."

"Give me a smoke, will you?"

She lit a cigarette and put it between his lips.

"Junction four," she said. "Ledgeworth's only a mile or two."

They drove on in silence, then he took the slow lane and decelerated. The motorway stretched ahead, bleak, wind-swept, running before them for a visible two miles. The traffic at that time in the afternoon was light.

"Just up here," he said. "We'll drop it up here."

"It?"

"The dog," he said impatiently.

"Harry. He's got a name."

"We must be quick," he said. "They can do you for stopping on the hard shoulder without good reason."

He got out and walked round to the nearside rear door. "Come on," he said.

The labrador got out of the car and stood on the tarmac, his hair blown up in patches by the wind which held the first signs of rain. His tail slapped the open door rhythmically, like a drum beat. He looked up at Malcolm with that patient certainty of which only dogs seem capable.

"There's a bit of a bank here," he said. Shrubs and a few young birch trees made an attractive background to the grass and flowering weeds which bureaucracy had not yet tidied up.

Angie did not get out of the car or look at him or Harry, but she put her arm out of the window and dangled a plastic bag.

44

"Here's the bone," she said. "Give him the bone up among the trees."

"Christ!" he said, "I must take its collar off."

"Why keep calling him 'it'?" she said irritably. "Here, give me the collar."

He took Harry up the short bank and gave him the bone under a birch tree, then walked quickly to the car. Angie was staring straight ahead with a far-away expression, as though her mind was elsewhere. He drove off through the slow and overtaking lanes, pushing the car to eighty five in a very few seconds. It was ten minutes before anything was said.

"Sandra would like a hamster," Angie remarked, as though continuing a conversation broken by deep thought. "Maybe that'd help."

"You don't think we should have done it, do you?" he asked truculently.

"It's what we tell the children that worries me."

"We tell them what we agreed. That we had to give it away."

"Him. Harry."

"Harry, then."

"They'll want good reasons."

"There are good reasons. They've got to learn the economic facts of life some time."

"I wish you hadn't given Kevin that fishing rod, so soon after the bicycle."

"You've got to encourage children if they show ability. Kevin's taken to fishing."

"It'll just make it more difficult for them to believe we couldn't afford to keep Harry any longer."

"Kids don't do those sort of sums. Anyway, we can't afford it. Him. Apart from what they'd have stung us for kennels, do you know what he's been costing us in food recently?"

"Of course I know. I do the shopping."

"Well, then. You could buy a bottle of Scotch for what it

45

takes to feed that dog for a week."

"We get through a bottle in three days; less when we have people in."

"So what are you saying?"

"We should never have bought him."

"It wasn't my idea. Anyway, we didn't buy him. The RSPCA people were lucky we took him off them. Labrador pups are two a penny."

"They did ask if we could afford to keep him, and you said 'yes'."

"You know what happened. Bricks, plasterboard, timber, all up as soon as I'd quoted for that schools job. Anyway, it was bloody cheek their asking."

"The girl said a lot of people take animals before Christmas, then get tired of them."

"It wasn't a question of getting tired of him. It's a matter of cost."

He flashed his headlamps at the car in front. "Get in the slow lane, you dozy sod."

"Don't go so fast; you're doing ninety."

"Look, after a few weeks' holiday the kids won't give Harry another thought. We've done it the right way."

"I heard his tail on the door. I wish he hadn't wagged his tail."

"For Christ's sake, Angie, stop working yourself up. He's probably eating steak on a stockbroker's settee in Ledgeworth by now."

"Or smashed to pieces by someone driving at this sort of speed."

His voice rose. "She'll do over a ton in perfect safety, so don't start on my driving."

"You just don't care, do you? About the children or about Harry or me or anyone."

"Christ! Thank you very much! Thank you very bloody much! I never *stop* paying out for this family. It was a new fridge last month, a whole new outfit for you to come away in, and if the hints I've been getting are anything to go by,

46

it'll be another video when we get back."

She knew his tempers and tried to calm him. "Life isn't all what you spend on things, Malc. It's . . . it's something more than that."

"From the way you lot consume, you could have fooled me. Anyway, what's suddenly turned you into a philosopher?"

"I just feel that somehow you . . . we . . . have begun to undervalue things."

"My impression is you value a nice home, a car, holidays, clothes, everything you want, bloody highly indeed."

"I didn't mean that. You bring everything down to money."

His patience snapped and he smashed his fist on the console.

"Jesus Christ!" he shouted. "It takes two to tango."

The rain was heavy now, coming out of a black sky.

"You'd better turn your lights on," Angie said.

He twisted the control savagely, his face lowering with resentment.

"Maybe you'd like to drive this car while you're about it?"

"Mother won't be fooled. You realise that, don't you?"

"Now what are you on about?"

"She'll guess about Harry."

"Your bloody mother would suspect the angel Gabriel if he turned up with a pools win."

"We should have told her. She might even have taken him."

"And complicate her trips to Benidorm and Majorca with an animal? He'd end up back with us each time, with me fetching and returning. No thanks."

"Do slow down, Malcolm. I can hardly see the road and the traffic's getting worse."

"Will you bloody stop driving this car?" he shouted. He turned on the stereo at full pitch, but without dropping speed.

47

Angie put her hands to her ears and screamed at him.

"Malcolm!! Slow down! Are you mad?"

The car was flashing under a series of bridges. The traffic volume foretold the great sprawl of the city that lay ahead. The road surface was a thin sheet of water that covered the car in hammering, blinding swathes each time they overtook a lorry in the centre lane. The motorway warning lights pulsed forty. Malcolm dropped to seventy, but the huge vehicle he had just passed, its shining tarpaulin sides bearing French wording, gave him a high-beam opinion of his road sense.

"Oh, shit yourself!" he yelled.

"Malcolm! For God's sake!"

So far as could be seen, the road ahead was clear. He accelerated again.

"Shut up!" he said viciously. His hands were clenched on the top of the steering wheel.

His wife's nerve broke completely. The din of the stereo above the roar of the engine and the thrashing rain overcame everything but fear. She raised Harry's collar, which she had been holding in her lap, and brought it down on Malcolm's left hand.

"Slow down!" she screamed. "You fool! You fool!"

They were approaching another bridge. Malcolm was so surprised by the pain of the collar's name disc on his knuckles that he looked round at Angie at the very moment that she screamed again.

"Stop! For God's sake, stop! There's a dog in the road."

It wasn't a dog, but they didn't know that until the car was locked into a skid and on top of the crumpled heap of sheeting lying in the outer lane. After that there was no time for accurate identifications. The car spun twice before hitting the structure of the bridge and bouncing off into the central lane. The Belgian vehicle behind was itself going nearer sixty than forty.

The police sergeant blew out his cheeks. Sustained

48

compassion is an emotion sometimes found in short supply among motorway police patrols.

"Blithering bloody idiots," he said objectively.

The young constable had been on motorway patrol long enough to share his superior's familiarity with such scenes. He ran his eye along the crushed concertina of jagged metal that had lately been a cherished motor car in Ford's upper range.

"What you reckon's the length of one of these, Sarge?"

The sergeant shrugged. "Fifteen feet? Fifteen and a half?"

"Can't be more'n eight or ten now. Wouldn't believe it, would you?"

"If you caught a fully-loaded container lorry up your backside, son, you'd believe anything except it was your birthday." He sniffed. "Especially if it was driven by some push-on wog."

The young constable poked gingerly into the small space that had been the passenger seat area. The ambulance men had had to take Angie out in handy pieces. He fished something from between the crushed seat and the twisted metal that might have been the door frame. It was a blood-soaked dog collar.

"Funny," he said. "No sign of a dog in there."

The sergeant made a face.

"Must have been *someone's* birthday, then," he acknowledged.

# The Man Who Loved Leopards

Old Douglas Henshaw was a bit of a rough diamond in his taciturn way, there's no denying. I suppose we hadn't a lot in common except for that prisoner of war camp in the forties. But after my wife died I met him in the Croydon Co-op, though it was only when he gave his name to the girl at the counter that I realised who he was. He had settled quite near me after retiring from his scrap metal business, so I looked him up and began to see him fairly often. I think he felt I didn't know anyone much, and I suppose he was right. Once Mary had gone I couldn't be bothered to keep up with the come-round-for-drinks brigade, and once the neighbours got the message that I wasn't interested in being a useful lone male for the local widows and fancy-free, I was left pretty well alone. Anyway, Douglas was as keen a draughts player as I am, which was what brought us together in the camp, and that's as good a basis for friendship as any.

Even so, I sometimes wonder if he would ever have told me about the leopard if Doris, his wife, hadn't happened to let it slip during one of their battles. Not that he *told* me much even then, any more than he told Doris.

"But there must be some reason why he wants to keep a leopard in the garden," I said to her once when he was out feeding it.

"Of course there is," she said crossly, almost as though she would have liked to blame me for the whole thing, "but I can't for the life of me get out of him what it is.

Sometimes I wonder if he isn't a bit, well, you know ... "
And she tapped her temple significantly.

Without being unkind, I suppose you could say Doris
was a little on the brassy side. Still a good-looking woman,
if rather over-weight, but too keen on the paintbox for my
taste. If she had given in and admitted that her hair was
grey, not the startling gold you were asked to believe, I
would have had more respect for her. But, poor woman, I
suppose she deserved some compensations. It was clear to
me, the outside observer, that the situation was beginning
to get her down. After all, not everyone wants a leopard in
their garden, not even if there is an obvious reason.

When I say "garden," by the way, don't get me wrong. I
don't mean some forty by ninety feet plot consisting of an
herbaceous border, a flowering cherry, a square of lawn,
and a small area for beans and rhubarb behind three feet
of privet.

No, indeed. Douglas Henshaw's garden was no simple
example of the surburban art of horticultural compression. Although surrounding what admittedly was a pretty
average kind of bungalow, it covered no less than ten
acres, almost all of it untamed woodland and a positively
encouraged tangle of bramble, thorn, wild rose, honey-
suckle and other prolific ingredients of an undergrowth
that advanced on the bungalow like a veritable jungle.

Jungle, perhaps, is the key word. Douglas had no
interest in gardens as such. It was jungle he was after.

"I think they let you read too much of that Kipling
man," Doris said on one occasion, meaning by "they" her
husband's long-dead parents.

"Don't be daft, Doris," Douglas replied, turning
over a page of "Wildlife Monthly", "I hadn't even heard of
Kipling until I left school."

"Well, whatever it was," Doris said firmly, "it's a great
pity it ever happened. Imprisoned we are by that wretched
animal. Imprisoned."

By this she meant they could never leave the place for

51

more than a few hours, while as for holidays, well that was something Doris had to be content to read about in travel agents' brochures. Stuffed with "far away", "two-centre," in-season and out-of-season offers their living room was. Not that Douglas showed the slightest interest. He'd done all the travelling he wanted years before, much of it in the army. Burma and so forth. It may have been something that happened out East that got him hooked on leopards, but that's only a guess.

Be that as it may, Douglas was for them, Doris wasn't, and that, as the Irish woman said, is where the trouble started.

Holidays apart, the mere cost of keeping the creature was horrific. It was not just a simple matter of having to face an enormous butcher's bill week in week out. There was no 'phoning the butcher and saying "Send a side of old cow or half a hundredweight of trotters." The meat had to be brought in from all sorts of different places, mostly a good way off, and the reason for this was the secrecy, which worried Doris stiff.

Douglas was a loner. Very independent. Hated red tape, bureaucracy, officialdom. This whole leopard thing had been done on the quiet. He had built the cage himself, having the bars made up by a blacksmith over fifty miles away. He smuggled them home by night, a few bars at a time, bolting them together by himself in the unseen centre of his private jungle.

Before making a cage to keep the leopard in, of course, he had to erect enough barbed wire to keep humans out, and it takes a lot of wire to enclose ten acres. Doris said it was like living in a concentration camp. But she was frantic about the secrecy. She wanted everything done above board, but he wasn't having any. Not just because he grudged the cost of the licence or was afraid the neighbours might object, but because he had his own ideas about how to keep leopards and didn't want any officious environmental-health pipsqueaks popping in every five minutes and checking on him. Besides, he might not even have got a licence, for keeping leopards is a suspect matter very properly covered by the Dangerous Wild Animals Act, and before a private individual can set up home with one of the big cats he has to give evidence of his experience and suitability. The local vet must also be in the picture and gets a fat fee for supervising the health and security aspects. In short, a District Council that for one reason or another is a bit jumpy about parcels of its district being turned over to jungle can make an awful lot of expensive trouble for the kind of person who is not keen on toeing the bureaucratic line. On the basis of "know thyself", Douglas had probably made the right decision.

But it did for his marriage. To start with, Doris was just fidgety and scratchy, like the leopard. Bit by bit she got a real hate on, first toward the leopard – though God knows the poor brute had never asked to be shut in a cage a stone's throw from Purley – and later toward Douglas. As their only close friend, I can tell you that bungalow had more snapping and snarling going on within its four walls than in any five square miles of average Asia.

She moaned a bit to me, of course, and I tried to see her point of view.

"I wish I could help," I said, "but Doug's not easy to reason with over things he cares about."

She sniffed. "Cares? I don't see much sign of it."

"I'm really sorry," I said. "For both of you. You and the leopard, I mean."

She sniffed again. "It gets its meals regular. I don't see it's much to complain about."

"All right," I agreed, glad to turn the topic away from Doris, "but a small cage in the middle of a Surrey garden isn't exactly a leopard's home from home."

"Where am I but in a cage?"

"At least you can get out from time to time. To the shops, the hairdresser."

"That animal wouldn't want to. Animals are different."

53

"I don't know," I said. "The more I see of zoos, the more I hate them. You should see the one in New York, in Central Park; the gorillas, the polar bears, the big cats; so listless and bored it'd make you weep."

"I can cry on that account without going to New York, thanks very much," she said. "People think too much about animals, not enough about humans. Humans come first."

"I doubt that's the point," I said. "I don't think we're going to behave much better toward each other until we've learned to treat other forms of life more decently. That man who said cruelty is indivisible made a major statement in very few words."

But I'd lost Doris who was rubbing at a china tiger with a duster as though she'd have liked to erase it.

Be that as it may, Douglas spent hours outside the leopard's cage in his deckchair, watching the animal pacing up and down or just lying around dozing. It had no company but Douglas and I'd guess it was bored out of its mind. Doris seldom went near it, and when she did there was no rapport. If that leopard was sensitive to vibrations, it had no feeling of being loved by Doris. I rather doubt that Douglas could be said to have loved it exactly, either, though he once said he did; maybe it was in a sense that one loves a steak or a lamb chop. He certainly liked owning it and being near it, and perhaps he got a kick from feeling he had beaten the system and was getting away with something no-one except Doris and myself knew anything about. But one could keep a rare stamp or a bit on the side on that basis, without love really entering into it.

For myself, I visited Douglas less and less often as the years went by. It was very depressing seeing the leopard getting older in that rusty iron cage. Douglas never made any real connection with the animal, either; not that I could see, anyway. I mean, you see pictures of people who keep big cats as pets, playing with them, taking them for walks, even sleeping with them. There was none of that with Douglas. All he wanted was to sit in his chair and watch his leopard pacing up and down, day in day out, while its coat got mangier, its eyes more dull, and the cage in its clearing grew darker year by year as the surrounding trees closed in above. I used to imagine a leopard's eye view from the cage, wondering what frustration or yearning there might be in its heart for the slats of blue sky, white cloud and green leaves that were all it knew of the world outside.

Mind you, leopards are mainly nocturnal, so maybe Douglas's poor beast did most of its speculating at night, but I can't be sure about that because I never saw it except in the daytime. Douglas said it had "adapted", by which I suppose he meant it shared his habit of being awake by day. It was a silent, sullen animal, as well it might have been, and I could never get out of Douglas whether it was incapable of roaring for some reason or other, or whether solitary leopards out of sight or smell of their own kind just don't have cause to be vocal.

What happened toward the end, of course, was that the animal fell sick. I was only surprised it hadn't happened sooner. Douglas was worried silly about this, but it was a classic case of being hoist with one's own petard. He couldn't enter the creature's cage and tend it, even if he knew what attention it needed. Doris, unsurprisingly, used it as a lever to get him to come out in the open and bring in the authorities, but he would have no truck with the idea.

"What would a bloody vet know, anyway?" he demanded. "All they understand is pussy cats and old dears' pekes. They'd have it shot within five minutes."

"They might take it to a zoo," Doris said. "Zoos must know about treating sick leopards."

"It'll get better" was Douglas's answer. "It's natural for an animal to be in health. It's probably been upset by condemned meat. I maybe shouldn't have got cheap horse

55

from that knacker."

And then he did what I found hard to take, but I dare say it was some sign of his depth of concern. He got some live dogs from a home for strays and shoved them into the cage, assuming that if the leopard killed its meat on the hoof, so to speak, it might be getting what it needed.

In the end, Doris could stand it no longer. The silly woman went down to the leopard's cage one night and opened the door, I suppose thinking it would be asleep and not likely to make its getaway until daybreak. She had no time to regret her mistake. It must have smelled her coming and crouched there in the dark. Anyway, it was through that door and on to Doris before she could have known what had hit her. In the morning Douglas found what was left of her body six feet from the cage, her head nearer nine. One of her legs was missing altogether. Of the leopard, not a trace.

At that point Douglas did several things, all of them ill-judged. Firstly, he made the assumption that the leopard, with a good meal in its belly, was resting up somewhere in the garden and would return to its cage out of habit and hunger in a day or two. Secondly, he buried Doris in a clump of gorse and birch where the soil was sandy and easy to dig. Thirdly, he went back to his bungalow and took various rather amateurish steps to make it seem Doris had gone away for an unspecified time. Then he sat back and waited for the leopard to return. It didn't. Days passed. He knew he had burned his boats, but he wasn't too worried. What he had not allowed for was that however carefully he kept the tragedy to himself, the abrupt disappearance of Doris must make some impact, however small, on third parties. She was known in the local shops; she had that gold hair done over once a week; she kept in touch with a few people by letter. Anyway, the police turned up eventually, didn't believe Doug's story, and within a few days had turned up Doris. She wasn't much

56

to look at by then, poor soul, and to the police the case was plain sailing.

Only then did Douglas admit that Doris had been killed by the leopard. What leopard, the police wanted to know. Well, this being a murder charge they went to a spot of trouble, going over every inch of those ten acres as well as scouring the surrounding countryside. There was no trace of a leopard, alive or dead.

I did what I could for Douglas, but I had been abroad when the disaster happened and didn't know a thing about it until I returned. By then he was behind bars, tried and sentenced. I went to the police, of course, and confirmed there had indeed been a leopard. But in the absence of the beast, and with the case closed, they preferred to assume I was a well-meaning friend prepared to perjure himself. I pointed out the cage, the barbed wire, the whole set-up, but they would not accept that as evidence. The seemingly hacked remains of a woman's body in three feet of sand were much less circumstantial.

So with Douglas's rather grudging agreement I tried to sell his bungalow so that he would have some capital to fight them with. But it was a bad time to sell and Douglas seemed to go off the idea. He appeared to have given up. Then one day I was down in the woodland at dusk, checking on the fences, when something hit me a nasty smack on the head. At first I thought it was a piece of branch from the tree above me, but when I bent down I saw it was a human shinbone. Its humanness didn't get through to me then and there, but the next day I went back with a triple extension ladder and got into the fork of the tree which was a real whopper with radiating branches making quite a platform thirty feet or more above the ground. There I found what I had suspected I would find, the remains of a leopard and some other bits and pieces that might have been Doris.

I thought Douglas should be the first to know. But all he said was "Oh, yes?" Just like that.

"But Doug," I said, "for Christ's sake, man, don't you see what this means? It'll get you out of here."

"Into what?" he said.

"Life," I said. "Freedom."

"They're relative terms," he said.

I couldn't believe my ears. "But look," I said, "you're not connecting with the facts. We can prove you are innocent."

"But I'm not, am I?" he said.

"Well, of course you are."

"Would Doris think so? The police? The district council? The leopard?"

"This is defeatist talk," I said.

He shrugged. In some strange way he seemed content.

"Thanks all the same," he said, "but it isn't worth the bother. I've made some kind of a life in this place. I'm reading more than I've ever read before. I don't see much point in fighting the system. Let's give them best."

I couldn't move him. I visited him twice more, then I gave up. In the end I concluded that that was what he really did want. But from time to time I lie awake at night gazing at the stars and trying to guess what frustration or yearning there might be in my friend's heart as he looks out from his prison cell at the slats of blue sky, white cloud and green leaves that are all he knows of the world outside.

# Monarch of the Glen

ONCE UPON a time there was a beautiful princess. She achieved that rank through marriage rather than by birth, for she was as pretty as a picture and could offer all those background attributes that enable princes to put the crucial question. Her father, an eighth earl, was Eton and Sandhurst and had been an equerry of the Queen, so they knew all about him at the Palace. There was a dissolved marriage in the background, it is true, but his clubs were right and his address was right, for the impressive if cold family home was plumb in the middle of the Shires.

It was there that the Prince had met her. More exactly, it was on a ploughed field within the grounds, for the shooting season was in full swing and the Prince, naturally, was shooting. It says something for the outward charms of the Earl's daughter that despite the not very glamorous attire that is proper to the slaughter of wildlife, the Prince that day only winged half his birds, so taken was he by the winsome presence of his host's charming girl. Normally at least seventy per cent of his birds died within a matter of minutes, for after a short lifetime of aiming guns at most of the socially acceptable living targets, he was a better shot than many of the people who by rank, brains or inordinate wealth had contrived to stand shoulder to shoulder with him in field and moorland. For two birds to be so poorly peppered as to fly on and become runners on a nearby estate, there to perish slowly from the fangs of non-human predators, was evidence of the degree of his distraction from the business in hand; for a pheasant whangs out of cover like an airborne tank, usually in a dead straight line at just the right height for sportsmen to be as sure as sportsmen can be of anything that they will return home visibly skilful and manly.

If any more assurance is needed that the Earl's daughter had made a tremendous impression on the Prince, his own words are on record, for as he said to his father within earshot of a servant, without parting his teeth and hardly moving his lips, "I do think she really is, I must say, most awfully pretty." It was probably the most strongly expressed confession of sensual susceptibility ever to have been forced into the open.

The marriage had the whole nation on the edge of its chairs. In the preceding weeks the country's ailing economy appeared to recover in a flurry of flags, postcards and unspeakably vulgar souvenirs. On the great day the entire populace was glued to The Box, women viewers revelling in the fashions and the personalities, strong men visibly moved by the bride's shy sidelong glances and dazzling if nervous smile. The bridesmaids were adorable, the weather was splendid, no-one seriously frightened the horses, and all in all it was a day fittingly summed up in the banner headline of one of the more staid newspapers which announced joyously WE HAVE A FAIRYTALE PRINCESS.

But the intensity of feeling was too strong to last. Even before the honeymoon was over, the nation sank back into sullen acceptance of being a declining power. The Prince returned to his routine of opening, inspecting, reviewing, travelling, and supervising the supervisors of his estates. He led a pretty busy life, even if the end product was somewhat intangible.

Sometimes the Princess was at his side, sometimes not. In certain respects she had been more popular with the media before marriage than after, as in those days it had been possible to portray her as a gentle, tender girl who liked nothing better than to look after small children in a Kensington nursery-school. So the media, who can be philosophical in these matters, settled back to wait until history might repeat itself.

It came, therefore, as something of a shock to a section of the nation when the Princess, who prior to marriage had been said to detest blood sports and even the wearing of furs, made a rotten job of shooting a Red Deer stag on her in-laws' estate at Malmoral. The beast, with its lower jaw shot away, made its escape and was not found for some hours. The servant who put it out of its misery unwisely reported its condition to someone who, so to speak, had danced with a man who had danced with a girl who had danced with someone from an animal-welfare organisation, and before long that section of the Press which for one reason or another is out of sympathy with the lifestyle of the royals painted a not very pretty picture of a not very pretty event.

Just why any realistic commoner should have been surprised by the Princess's apparent volte-face is, however, difficult to understand. If not technically obliged to obey her husband, the spirit of any true marriage is that you take it on for better or for worse, and there was nothing in her upbringing likely to prompt rebellion against such sound conventions. As the Prince himself had said without parting his teeth, "I do think, don't you know, that it really would be most awfully appropriate if you were to be seen with me on all, as it were, appropriate occasions." Any small reservation there might have been in his bride's pretty head about staying her soft young hand from the fun slaying of certain species was rapidly quashed by the appeal to duty. Besides, her mother-in-law herself was a notable destroyer of deer life, so it might have been construed as not only disloyal but as positively bad manners for the Princess to have abstained. To those who at this

61

point may cite other values, let them remember that while it may be the prerogative of the great to be merciful, to be a royal is not necessarily or by definition to be great in each and every sense of that word. Is it not the sheer humanity of great people that enables their lesser brethren to identify with them?

In any case, girls reluctant to taste the joys of granting to other species early release from life's vicissitudes do not as a rule appear on ploughed fields in the company of shooters during the pheasant season. Most of them, also, do not go out of their way to marry princes whose chief form of amusement, like that of their families, has long been the pursuit of game. Possibly the Princess had been confused by her father-in-law's presidency of the Royal Society for the Conservation of Wildlife, but then she was a young and rather innocent creature who could not reasonably be expected to know that those who show concern for the survival of sub-human species have it in mind to conserve them for their own use and pleasure, not through any muddled notion that lesser life forms should enjoy some ill-defined right to existence except by courtesy of God's greatest creation.

Love, it has been said, is all. In royal circles this cannot be so. Custom and duty come first. This explains why the Prince and his family had early and thoroughly gone to work to eradicate from the Princess's emotional repertoire any conceivable twinge of sentimentality or reservation about such time-honoured pursuits as healthful field sports. The very idea that some latent spark of squeamishness might have prompted so socially interruptive a gesture as refusal to participate in the wide range of sporting pleasures for which the royal family had for generations done its level and successful best to set the standard, was quite unacceptable. It is easy to see why. Taken to its logical – one is tempted to say illogical – conclusion, any such tendency could extend its tentacles as far even as the royal stables, threatening the whole range of horse-centred activities which had long been the only obvious source of enjoyment for the Queen herself. That, it must surely be agreed, would not have done.

For some while, therefore, the media, quietly conscious of the unspoken rules in such delicate areas, maintained an acceptable balance between the unwise extremes of portraying the Princess either as a trigger-happy member of an insensitive elite, or as a caring but unrealistically soft-hearted candidate for motherhood and eventual succession. If it could not safely be omitted from a press report that the Princess had accompanied her husband on one of his manly forays, any possibility of public disquiet was stilled by such tactful phrases as that "the Princess was believed to be one of the party." Needless to say, the Leftist papers and the contemptible minority organs that catered for old women and the cranks who raise objections to the sporting reduction of other species were less inclined to join this mild conspiracy, but then it never has been and doubtless never will be possible to do much about the Leftist press and the lunatic fringe. They are part of the cross which the establishment has learned over the years to bear.

Before very long, as might have been expected and indeed was, the union was strengthened by the birth of a son. The media refocused joyfully on the Princess as mother rather than wife. It was easier and more agreeable for the public to identify with her role as parent, so the sportswoman image was given decreasing attention. Besides, little William made a much more cuddly picture than untidy shots of men and women pointing guns at blurred targets against nebulous skylines.

Within a few years William acquired a sister, Louise. She was a bright, bouncy baby and grew rapidly into a mischievous little girl who seemed to be shaping up into an altogether livelier character than her brother, who from the word go had been carefully trained to accept all that the royals and their retinue regarded as normal behaviour.

So William and Louise, by now well accustomed to the sporting habits of their elders, were to be seen on a certain memorable day in early winter at their grandparents' estate in the Highlands. As a special treat they had been allowed to accompany their family and friends on a stalking expedition. This was particularly agreeable to little William because that very day his father had told him he was old enough to be entrusted with the air gun whose supervised use had played such a part in giving backbone to his education. A rather fine gun, it was made finer by the box of improved pellets thoughtfully given by William's great uncle. The pellets were the air gun manufacturer's answer to the dum-dum rifle bullet that expands as it passes through a body, leaving a wider area of devastation at the point of exit than entrance. As the Duke had said to the Prince, "It'll make the boy feel he's getting somewhere." This was very true, for so many creatures escape to die in wasteful privacy after being merely wounded by the conventional pellet. As the Prince accurately predicted without parting his teeth, "I do think that William really will be most terribly appreciative of your gift."

So William, of course debarred from joining the actual stalkers, was well content to lag behind in the hope of a chance to pot at any small birds or mammals he might encounter on the fringe of the rearguard party. A splendid feature of his gun was its relative silence.

Then suddenly . . . excitement! News came through that the Prince had shot a splendid stag. Young William, who so far had only been able to dream of getting in his sights the monarch of the glen, was wild with delight, jumping up and down and thirsty for details of the creature's size and antlers. The servant who brought the news could not supply this data, and it was then that Louise suggested a very naughty thing indeed.

"Come on, William," she whispered, "let's go and see for ourselves."

William looked doubtful. "Do you think we should?" he said.

"Of course we shouldn't," Louise replied impatiently and with that slight lisp that had made her tender years the more endearing, "that's what makes it fun."

By first disappearing behind a Range Rover it was not too difficult to slip away through the conifer plantation without being seen by the servants or those too aged or uninvolved to be where the action was.

Once among the trees William adopted the stance and concentration of a stalker, holding his gun low to the ground and crouching as he ran from tree to tree until they found themselves on the far side of the dark plantation and in open ground that ran up to a small peak of rock. They were alone. Gloriously, rarely alone.

"Come on!" William shouted excitedly. "You are *slow*, Louise."

With sudden inspiration he dropped his gun and ran up to the rocky peak, then bending forward he put his wrists to each side of his head and extended his fingers in puny imitation of the antlers of a stag.

"Look!" he cried. "Look at me! I'm a great red stag."

Louise, following as fast as her shorter legs permitted, giggled and waved.

"Oh, William," she said, "you are silly!" She picked up his gun.

"I'm not silly," William said proudly. "I'm the greatest, finest stag that has ever been seen."

"All right," said Louise, happily entering into the spirit of the game, "you're a huge big marvellous stag and I'm a great wonderful hunter just like daddy."

She ran towards her brother, waving the air gun and laughing, while William raised his antlered head and emitted the deep bellow of a fine big stag.

In the weeks that followed no-one suggested it had been anything but a ghastly accident. And indeed it had not. Louise's devotion to her brother was unquestionable. Had she not tripped on the gnarled root of heather growing from the rock, the media and the country at large would happily have been deprived of one of the most harrowing stories ever sparked off by the private life of the royals. It had been a chance in ten thousand that the pellet that hit William should not only have shot the lad's lower jaw away, but should have so shattered a main artery that he bled to death before his horrified sister had been able to bring help.

The country mourned. The Prince and the Princess were little pestered by the media for several weeks, and when once again they were seen returning to the social round they were invariably given the greatest coverage when opening children's homes or hospital wings. The associations were very agreeable to the public mind.

It is some indication of how deeply the tragic incident was felt by all concerned that a spring, a summer and half an autumn passed before the Prince was seen to have returned to the consolations of a sporting life in the Highlands. As for the Princess, another whole year went by before it was even suggested that she might be a member of any of the Prince's shooting parties. These matters can be handled with great delicacy by those who know how to behave.

# Mistral

If you know the South of France (what most people mean by the South of France, that is – the Côte d'Azur), you may know St Tropez. But maybe not. Users of what is loosely called the Riviera are extraordinarily insular. Even with the autoroute – perhaps because of it – the country west of the Esterel is as foreign to many who favour the region to the east, as Perth is to Penzance.

But not to me. I have seen all I want of the French coast from Marseilles to Menton, and you can have Nice, Monte Carlo and the rest with a pound of tea. They have nothing on St Trop.

I am prejudiced, of course. Partly, perhaps, because enjoyment of today's Côte d'Azur is an art, not a choice easily bought by casual application to the tour operators. Nowhere along that expensive littoral is it more essential to exercise that art than in the area of St Tropez. Where Cannes and Monaco have something to offer at almost all times of the year, St Trop demands from the visitor the approach, the reverence, of the connoisseur.

In high summer, for instance – the most popular and unsuitable period – you need to be a rabid *bon vivant*, a truly person person, to endure the sheer excess of humankind in a region offering no outlet for urban overspill. In the winter, on the other hand, none but a misanthropic masochist with an inordinate concern not to miss the first golden promise of mimosa is going to suffer the bleak desolation of empty streets so often scoured by that most unpleasant of God's varied gifts, the mistral.

"Unpleasant", for many, is putting it mildly. Some, the purists – those likely to hold that the Riviera lies only between Nice and Genoa – say that nowhere west of Cap Ferrat is really habitable, so frightful is that cold dry wind that roars down the Rhône valley to spread its fury over Provence, proving to pursuers of the *dolce vita* that Nature alone is truly egalitarian. Others, less hysterical, chance wintering in Cannes and Antibes. But further west, beyond the Esterel, there you have to know what you are about. There you have to have some special reason for defying the natural and man-made perils so inadequately repelled by the Massif des Maures.

One of those special reasons, of course, is the concentrated pulchritude of St Trop. Not only are its summer girls beautiful and plentiful, but they show a lack of inhibition less apparent in such self-conscious resorts as Cannes and Nice than on the cleaner beaches and the open waters of St Trop. Not for nothing has that delightful little town so long been the haunt of writers, artists and the least stuffy of media persons.

Even a few miles down the coast in Port Grimaud, that pseudo-Venetian aqua-suburb for retired civil servants and bank managers from Croydon and St Cloud, nubile girls still with ponies in Surrey meadows, bare their breasts the moment they set foot on golfe-bound yacht or motor boat.

Be that as it may, the last person I expected to meet there, even in June, was Ambrose. One of the connoisseur months, June is a little ahead of the worst of the mob, a time when one can sit at a café table in the Place des Lices, enjoying the cool shade below the huge plane trees, listening early and late to the click of boules, watching through the hotter hours those who forsake the quayside and the expensive refreshments at Senequiers to explore the quieter streets and squares. In June, before the French rush like lemmings to the coast, the weather can

68

be exquisite. But in no month of the year can one be sure of avoiding the mistral.

Ambrose had not seen me. His gaze was on the dry brown powdered earth of the square. His shoulders were more stooped than I remembered, his expression verging on the gloomy. Seeing that he was literally attached to the sexiest woman I had seen in years, this seemed odd.

"Hey! Ambrose!" I called.

He looked up.

"Oh, hallo, Charles," he said. His voice lacked animation, let alone surprise. Our last meeting might have been five days back, not five years.

"I didn't know this was your beat and season," I said.

He compressed his lips and wrinkled his brow in a facial shrug. He certainly looked older, but except for an unremembered scar on his neck, much the same dapper, neat little man a head shorter than myself.

"It's not really," he said, "but Angelina likes the warmth."

I smiled, feeling that introduction was called for. On the few occasions we had met since schooldays, Ambrose had invariably been accompanied by beautiful women, none of whom he had married so far as I knew. I had never known him well – he was too much of a woman's man for that – and if it had not been for the school link I might not have numbered him among remembered acquaintances. As with relations, those one has known at school are not necessarily the people one keeps up with.

"Well, have a drink," I said.

Ambrose introduced me. "This is Charles Massingham. Charles, meet Angelina." He gave her no second name.

Angelina offered me a slim, brown hand. Her wrists bore several thin gold bangles and her nails were painted the tawny brown of dried blood. She did not grip my hand, yet I felt through her fingers a strange, urgent strength, and this was apparent in the way she moved. Her figure was flawless, her body extraordinarily supple. I wondered if she was a dancer. She wore a bronze-gold jump-suit that fitted her perfectly, emphasizing the spareness, the alert animality of her body. Her long legs – like me, she was inches taller than Ambrose – were flattered by fine high-heeled gold sandals that must have cost the earth, and her black hair was drawn back from a face that was more feline than human, though of exquisite delicacy and proportion. The only imperfection, though it detracted nothing from her sensuality, was a slightly over-full lower lip, imparting a faint air of smouldering challenge. She reminded me of one of the great cats – a cheetah, perhaps. This impression was strengthened by the fine chain leash that was attached to her left wrist and held by Ambrose, for all the world as though he were walking an Afghan or Saluki.

I carefully avoided a second glance at the gold leash. Ambrose had always enjoyed getting reactions from those more unimaginative and staid than himself. Even at school, in the days when I was far more interested in The Boys' Own Paper and the egg-laying habits of peewit and sparrow-hawk than in the thin dark ice of human relationships, Ambrose was a living legend to the older boys. In fact, his precocity did little for his formal education, for having made it in the shrubbery with St Bartholomew's singularly pretty matron, he was expelled without a moment's hesitation by the matron's husband, who as it happened was the headmaster, and never got round to taking the exams that might have channelled his energies toward university, a solid job, and a more serious lifestyle. To make matters worse, his father died about then, leaving investments and property that provided his son with an all too adequate income for the rest of his life. Riches and randiness: a heady combination few survive.

I had reached that time of life when, meeting a beautiful woman, I could take her or leave her, so to speak. Well, leave her, then, without actually taking. You know what I mean. But I had to admit that Angelina was some-

70

thing special. She sat at the table almost gingerly, as though unaccustomed to a chair, so lightly in contact with it that I felt she might have sprung away through the plane trees at the slightest provocation – had it not been, of course, for that slender gold leash. Her eyes were watchful, never still; alert, restless, seeking. Yet seeking what?

"Well," I said unimaginatively, "this is quite a surprise."

"For me too," said Ambrose. "I didn't suppose you still came out here."

"I'm flattered you've considered the matter," I said.

The waiter appeared.

"What will you have?" I asked.

"Angelina likes orange juice. The real thing. I'll have the same."

Angelina seemed to accept this choice.

"What do you want in it?" I asked Ambrose.

"Nothing. Just as it comes."

I blinked. I had never known Ambrose drink anything non-alcoholic. Even at school he had a reputation for rather good wines. "Clarets, dear boy," I remember him saying as we waited to bat in some house match, "are really the best for your digestion. Go for the Médocs and you will have little trouble." It never struck me in those days that his sophistication could be anything but innate.

"Right," I said, and ordered.

Angelina stroked Ambrose's arm with her free hand and looked into his eyes. Except for a murmured " 'Allo" when we shook hands, I had not heard her speak.

"I mus' go hawaii for lily time," she said mysteriously.

"Must you?" Ambrose replied. "Very well, then; come straight back."

I had noticed the small key on the fine chain round his neck, and now he used this to unfasten the little padlock that held the leash to the lowest and most robust of the bangles on Angelina's wrist. She slid silently from her

71

chair and disappeared into the cool depths of the café.

"Italian?" I asked.

"Hungarian with a dash of Spanish."

"Some mix!"

I clenched my fist, grimacing, and punched the air, holding my forearm rigid in a gesture familiar to men, but one I had not used for many years. Ambrose nodded. The old animation had definitely gone.

"I know what you're thinking. She's not all body, though."

"No?"

"No. You may not believe it, but she has a lovely nature. Very tender-hearted. Wouldn't hurt a fly. Loves animals. We were with Brigitte only yesterday."

"Bardot?"

He nodded. "She's intelligent too. Quite a thinker. Angelina, I mean."

"Well, you never know," I said.

"She's very environmentally sensitive."

"Really? Low technology? Alternatives?"

"Population control especially. She thinks our numbers should be drastically reduced until we have small communities living only in suitable climatic areas."

"Not the kind of thing the politicians would want to follow up," I said.

The waiter brought their orange juices.

"Are you quite sure you'd like nothing stronger?" I said. "Before Angelina returns. A little gin, perhaps?"

He shook his head. "I've made a deal."

"Who with? Alcoholics Anonymous?"

"With Angelina."

"She doesn't look the type to exert a reforming influence."

"As you said, 'you never know'."

"Well," I agreed, "it's probably no bad idea to watch things a bit once one's in sight of one's fifties."

"That's what Angelina says. She says she wants me fit

72

or not at all."

"You don't think," I said, "that in this climate, with a girl like that, at our sort of age . . . ?"

Ambrose gestured, a little impatiently.

"It's an attitude of mind, Charles. You've given up too soon."

"Not given up exactly," I replied. "I'm still married to Christine."

"Well, there you are. We make our beds."

I changed the subject.

"Are you ever in London?"

"Seldom. Last July, for two weeks, but we move around. Angelina won't winter in Europe. It has to be the Caribbean, the Seychelles – that kind of thing."

"An expensive girl."

"But worth it. I could tell you . . . "

"Don't. I may have given up, as you put it, but the heat still turns one on a little."

"I'm glad to hear it," Ambrose said. "Angelina thrives on heat. She says we were intended for sub-tropical temperatures. That was what I was about to tell you. She really has a most enquiring mind."

"But the other side . . . ?" I enquired. "Surely . . . ?"

"Of course. That too. But there's another face to the coin, you know, Charles. Sex isn't everything."

"No," I said. "No, indeed. How true."

The conversation flagged. The waiter, hopeful, handed me the menu. I looked at my watch. Ambrose looked at his, then toward the dark interior of the café.

"Seeing to her face," he said.

"It's getting on. How about lunch here? It's adequate."

Ambrose glanced at the menu.

"I don't know there's much for us."

"Steak?" I suggested. "Veal? The fish isn't bad."

"We . . . I . . . don't eat like that any longer," he said.

"Problems?"

I'd had some myself. All part of the aging process.

Mushrooms and sweet corn seemed immune to the digestive juices.

"Not really. More a . . . reorientation."

"You could have an omelette."

"Do they do a good salad?"

"I'm sure they *could*," I said. "What about the cold plate?"

Ambrose came out with it.

"We don't eat meat."

My memory was that he ate little else.

"There really have been some changes," I said.

"Angelina feels it's for our own good. Meat doesn't suit her. She's for whole food, grains, fruit, nuts – that kind of thing. She says it's as necessary we eat the right things as that we don't live in cold climates."

"Why so much concern about the cold? Do you catch chills easily?"

"No, but Angelina is – how shall I say? – better adjusted in the heat. Warmth and a bland diet are what she needs. The cold prompts her to eat things that, well, disagree with her. When the mistral blows, we stay indoors."

"It all sound a trifle restricting," I said.

A worried look crossed his face.

"It *can* be a bit of a strain, actually. Angelina needs constant encouragement to . . . be herself."

"Nasty wind, the mistral," I agreed, not quite knowing what to say about his last remark. "Gets into the bones. The sirocco can be unpleasant, too, and I'm told people can go potty in that wind they get on the northern slopes of the Alps."

"The föhn," Ambrose said. "They call it the chinook in the Rockies. It cools at the saturated adiabatic lapse rate as it reaches the peaks, then dries as it descends on the leeward side, gaining heat."

"I've never heard it better put," I said.

He nodded. "Mind you, 'it's an ill wind . . . ' Angelina really turns on in the mistral."

"You mean . . . ?" I said.

He nodded again. "All I can handle until it gets warmer again."

"Here she comes," I said.

Angelina's jump-suit was more open than before, exposing a delicious area of brown skin and just enough of each plump breast to . . . well, never mind: it was one o'clock and very warm indeed. She approached slowly, like a cautious cat not wanting to draw attention to herself. As she sat down she extended her arm submissively toward Ambrose who attached the chain to her wrist. I wondered what the women's libbers would have thought about it all. I noticed that her nostrils were dilating and contracting gently, like an animal scenting its prey. Although she had walked only a few yards, she was panting quietly, her small pink tongue a little extended. She was wildly beautiful – and I mean 'wildly' despite that submissive act to Ambrose. Old and almost forgotten tremors threatened to disturb my peace of mind. I shifted on my chair.

"So how long are you here, Charles?" Ambrose enquired, toying with the *crudités* the waiter had brought with a promptness suggesting no special preparation.

"Another week. July and August are unbearable. Besides, I hate to miss the English summer in our cottage. The scabious will be flowering on the Downs soon – the most beautiful colour in the world. With the corn ripening, the real woods to walk in . . ."

"You were always a one for nature," Ambrose said. "At your own level."

"Well, here it's all over. Nature is resting. Don't you miss England in spring and summer? The larks? The cowslips?"

He nodded. "I suppose so. One certainly knows where one is with cowslips."

"I can't think what one would do out here," I said, "once everything dries up and the trippers descend like locusts. The sailing fraternity tests the *savoir vivre* of the

75

most gregarious."

"I read a lot," Ambrose said.

"That's another change in you, then," I said. "You were always too busy doing . . . other things."

"One matures," Ambrose said.

"What do you read? Bond stories? Agatha Christie?"

"Not often. More, reincarnation, Eastern religious thought."

"Good God!" I said.

A sudden swirl of air swept through the Place des Lices, a welcome disturbance of the almost solid heat, yet a warning of less pleasant things to come. I looked up from my plate at Angelina, for I thought I had heard a sharp indrawing of breath. She was gazing up at the rustling leaves of the plane trees, her fork poised above her plate, her nostrils contracting and dilating again, but more forcefully than before. Her food looked so dull – just raw vegetables and a small portion of cream cheese.

"Do you never eat meat?" I asked her.

She shook her head slowly.

"She hasn't for a very long time," Ambrose said. "She probably couldn't even keep it down now."

"Is that right?" I asked Angelina. "It would make you sick?"

She shrugged and grimaced, a half smile making her face even more enchanting.

"Here," I said, "see if Ambrose is right."

I sliced a corner off my steak and offered it to her on the knife's point. It was rarer than I really enjoy. She allowed me to place it between her parted lips, and I noticed how sharp and slightly retracted her white teeth were as they closed on the meat. I felt she was being polite rather than of a mind to undergo the test, but she chewed obediently, reflectively, finishing it sooner than I expected. I cut another piece.

"More?" I said.

She took it willingly enough, then another. At the fifth

piece Ambrose looked alarmed.

"Steady. That's enough. You know it's not good for you, Angelina."

Her eyes turned from mine to his, her smile disappearing. She chattered to him, fast, in what I took was Hungarian, her eyes burning, her lips hardly moving.

"It's still appallingly hot," I said. "Why don't you come back to my villa for coffees? It's cooler up in Gassin. I'm due for drinks on a gin palace in the port, so I can run you back later."

"I'd like that," Ambrose said.

His instant acceptance surprised me. As I say, we had never been close, yet I felt he was quite glad we had met up again. Angelina seemed less keen. She stroked his arm and looked into his eyes, speaking with her own rather than in words, though from her throat came a strange pleading noise that was almost a purr. But all he said was: "Just for a little while."

In the car he started to talk about reincarnation, asking me my views on transmigration and karma. I said I had not thought much about them, which was true. I noticed the scar on his neck reddened as he warmed to the subject.

I had taken the villa from friends who escape the mixed blessings of the Côte d'Azur from June until September. It was beautifully situated to the west of the village, with a fine view of the main range of the Massif. The terrace was a mass of oleanders and geraniums, with nothing beyond but the far hills across the falling wasteland of ilex, cork-oak, pine and scrub. The breeze was more positive and cooler than in town, but as yet not so strong as to be uncomfortable. I sat Ambrose and Angelina in the cushioned chairs and went inside to make coffee.

When I reappeared with the tray, all was clearly not well. They were quarrelling in low tones and Angelina was pulling against her leash, her eyes flashing, her extraordinary nostrils registering more than her words, which were unintelligible.

"Charles, I'm sorry, but I think we'll have to leave," Ambrose said. "Angelina's rather unhappy about this wind."

"I hoped you'd enjoy the coolness," I said.

"That's the problem. Below a certain temperature she's never quite herself, and the mistral demands certain measures . . . I think we really must get back. Our villa's very warm and sheltered."

"Of course," I said. "I'm sorry you have this difficulty."

"And we're sorry about the coffees."

"I tell you what," I said. "Take my car. I've friends in Gassin who are going into St Trop this afternoon, and I've some shopping to do before the party. They can pick me up. If you leave the car in the Place des Lices, I can collect it later. I'll show you where to leave the keys."

Ambrose didn't let Angelina off her leash, even in the driving seat. Because of my car's right-hand drive, he had to switch wrists so that she could sit beside him. He made sure the passenger door was locked, then told her to get in across the driver's seat. She was very restless, almost fearful, and made sounds from her throat that were even less like speech than those she made before. I could see that Ambrose was tense and worried. It was quite a relief when they drove off down the winding minor road toward the N98.

Tony and Janet Turner seemed glad to give me a lift. They had their own problems, mostly of trying to keep together an unsatisfactory marriage by a frequent change of geography. They were rich enough to keep four small properties in different parts of the world, and they spent about three months in each. Others' company broke up their bickering. As we drove toward St Tropez, the car rocking in the wind that now howled between the hills, I told them something about Ambrose and Angelina.

"I think we've met them," Janet said. "Yes, I'm sure we

78

have. In Grimaud, at the Brothertons'. He's short, very smooth."

"Bit of a lady-killer," Tony said. "I remember. The girl was absolutely terrific."

Janet sniffed. She did a lot of sniffing. "That depends on your taste in such matters."

I was sideways on and slightly to the rear of Tony's grin.

"I think she could be quite a handful," I said.

"Mmmmm," Tony agreed lasciviously, gripping the steering wheel hard enough to drive the blood from his fingers.

"There's something almost . . . untamed about her," I said.

Janet sniffed again. "Pretty near to the jungle, if you ask me."

I leaned forward from the rear seat, peering through the windscreen.

"My God!" I said. "That's my car."

It had been, anyway. What I now owned looked destined for the scrap-yard. It was piled up against the concrete wall of a storm pipe that ran under the road, on a nasty little bend.

Janet paled. "Maybe they're still in it. Maybe no-one's been along."

"Then for Christ's sake, woman," Tony said, "we must do something about it."

The car was empty, the steering wheel bent, the windscreen shattered, the bonnet concertinad. Some drops of blood on the dashboard and the driver's seat were still tacky.

"If police or ambulance had been, they'd have left warning notices," I said. "Or someone on guard until the recovery truck arrived."

Janet frowned. "Then where are they?"

"God knows," I said. "They only left forty minutes ago. Look, I'm sorry, I think you'd better go on without me. I feel I should make a search. They may have been injured and wandered off in a daze."

"We'll help," Tony said. "Of course."

"Then perhaps Janet could stay in the car in case anyone comes by," I said.

The road was steep and the land sloped away from it, a maze of wild scrub and underbrush with occasional pines and outcrops of rock.

"It's no spot to be lying out with injuries," Tony said. "Least of all in this bloody wind."

"If you'll take the area to the south," I said, "I'll work north from the cars. Perhaps if we cover the ground in parallel strips . . . "

After twenty minutes I found a piece of Ambrose's shirt. A little further on I found Ambrose. I recognised him by his shoes; much the same bracket as Angelina's. Where his nose and eyes had been was a fly-inviting quagmire of blood and torn skin. A missing ear had left an untidy hole that oozed gently into the mica-speckled shale of the rocky hollow in which he lay. His light clothing seemed to have been torn from his body, and I saw that all the smaller (I don't say minor) extremities were missing. As for his throat, it was simply not there; only a hideous gape of raw flesh with a protuberance of gristle I took to be his Adam's apple. I am not a squeamish man, but the undigested remains of my Place des Lices luncheon ended up in the scrub-oak near Ambrose's mangled left hand. Of Angelina and the leash there was nothing to be seen.

Nor was she ever found. I have often pondered on the incident, wondering what it was that Ambrose might have told me had we had longer together; recalling his untypical interest in Eastern beliefs, his apparent knowledge of the strange winds that can wreak such changes in human temperament; Angelina's animal restlessness; those glimpses of something not susceptible to normal explanation.

But then mine is not a psychic or complicated nature. I prefer rational explanations to over-imaginative speculation. Nevertheless, when the wind gets up and I am alone – and that is most of the time now that Christine has died and I come out to Gassin more often – I go out on to the terrace and look across to the distant hills of the Maures. And something in me tells me to walk off into the scrub in search of Angelina, who I know cannot possibly still be there. And something else in me, which invariably wins, tells me to come indoors, to close the windows and the shutters, and to lose myself in my books until the mistral has blown itself out.

I've become quite absorbed in Eastern ideas, incidentally. Reincarnation, karma, that kind of thing. From a purely intellectual standpoint, of course.

# St Martin's Summer

H E PUSHED the deck chair deep into the tangle of briar and dried bracken. The rug followed, then the small flat bottle of gin. He would bring the rest the next day, when it was Sylvia's turn to have the car and she would be dropping him for his walk, saving a mile of boring road work.

"Come on, Roddy," he said. "Homies."

So that was it. Ready to go. As he walked back to the car, keeping his balance on the rutted woodland path by stabbing touches of his stick, he went through the details once again. Meticulous, he knew he had made no mistakes, forgotten nothing. But this was the big one, as Kojak used to say; a little extra thought was justified.

Ahead, the labrador snuffled eagerly, erratically, his nostrils tantalized by rabbit, squirrel and the plentiful pheasants that ran, whirred and rattled out of their path. So early in the shooting season the woods were alive with the fat, sleek birds, timid and indignant at such disturbance after many weeks of being pampered and hand-fed by the gamekeepers.

The car was a mile and a half down the lane and across two fields. As was usual on this lonely part of the Downs, they had met no-one. Before his leg had begun to play up, they could walk for five or six hours without seeing a soul. Even at weekends a few hundred yards would shake off all but the most dedicated leisure-users.

He was not sorry to sink into the driving seat. It had

been taxing to carry bits and pieces up the hill over cattle-churned fields and the rough-surfaced bridleway. On the dull cold day, the Aga-warmed kitchen was a welcome prospect.

Sylvia had bought a packet of crumpets. They had two each for tea.

Ever since he had planned this day he had wondered whether he would go through with it. Not only whether, but how. Saying good-bye to Sylvia, for instance, for what she could not guess was the last time.

When it came to it, it was much like any other day. It had to be. Only the business of not taking Roddy was out of step.

"He'll be rather disappointed," Sylvia said. "Such lovely weather, too. Almost like September. Yesterday I thought winter had arrived."

"I know. But it's better I go alone. I do want to get up to the folly again while I still can, and there are so many pheasants up there."

"He wouldn't kill any, surely?"

"It's the disturbance. I promised Rogerson."

"You must take him with you to-morrow, then. You've never left him behind before."

"Of course."

So she dropped him at the bottom of Puck's Lane, a mile from where he had driven the previous day. That was part of his plan. From Puck's Lane she would not imagine him cutting across country to pick up a route that for years had been quite a different walk. It would postpone discovery enormously.

He said "See you later," and she smiled and drove off just as on any other day when she dropped him. He watched the Mini out of sight, perhaps slightly hot behind the eyes, but strangely calm.

Unsurprisingly, the things were still there. Few spots on

the Downs were more remote. Opposite the plantation of beech, oak and ash of greater age had given most of their leaves to the bridleway's carpet of brown and gold which the strengthening sun would crisp into giant cornflakes before the November day was done. He felt guilt at denying Roddy his walk, missing his company. The dog's joy in dried leaves was like that of a small boy.

The rug seemed quite dry, despite the light rain that had fallen in the night. Wouldn't do to get a chill . . . With a faint smile he tucked the rug under one arm, pocketed the gin bottle and picked up the chair. Then he walked a hundred or so yards to the north before taking the almost indiscernible deer track through the plantation. After a few minutes he was into older woodland, picking his way over fallen branches and whole trees that had lain there for years, of no concern to the foresters. Great beeches, many years beyond their commercial span of life, stood in forgotten splendour, most gaunt with the limb loss of old age, and here and there the dark spread of unimaginably older yews lent a sombre, timeless feel to this neglected corner of the forest.

He reached a moss-covered bank made of flints thrown up centuries before, perhaps as a boundary. Its age was confirmed by the occasional beech tree which topped the bank, erosion exposing massive roots now so barked as to resemble ground-level limbs. He walked up the bank and down into the already sun-warmed hollow on its far side. He had arrived.

The hollow was on the fringe of the forest, facing south over a downward slope of rabbit-cropped turf almost encircled by the forest. Too steep ever to have been disturbed by the plough, in high summer it harboured plants rarely encountered elsewhere on the Downs.

The view was magnificent, taking in some twenty-five miles of coastline, beyond which the sea shimmered through the haze drawn by the sun from the drying turf. A rich man with a soul – if that was no contradiction – would

84

have paid a fortune to be allowed to build his house in such a spot.

He had found it years before, when Roddy was a pup. Apart from coming across a snare set on the edge of the woodland, he had seen no sign of human life within half a mile. He was confident that on a November weekday he need not fear interruption. He looked at his watch. On schedule.

He set up the deckchair, then covered it with the rug, but it was too warm in the sheltered hollow to bother with wrapping it round himself. For a few minutes he lay back with his eyes closed, enjoying the sun on his face, then shook his head, realizing he might doze off. Every colour was sharper, every shape more clear, for having shut his eyes against the morning sun. A few yards to the west the deeply grooved trunk of an oak was briefly visited by a small grey bird that probed into its recesses. A leafless hawthorn covered in old man's beard, the sun behind it, might have been a cherry tree in blossom.

He removed the flask from his jacket, also another smaller bottle, propping them beside the chair against a fallen branch from the beech above. Then he took out a pen and an envelope, removing two sheets of writing paper. He propped them, half folded, against the back of his open wallet to give enough firmness for writing.

Sylvia, old girl, I'm sorry about this, but it seemed the best way. We feel the same about ending up on some geriatric ward, so I think and hope this won't be too much of a shock for you. I'm afraid it's going to put a few people to some trouble and expense, but not as much as having me lying around in hospital fighting their determination to keep me a well-behaved vegetable. That as you know is the one prospect that has ever really scared me.

The doc's report last week wasn't too good. Could be six months, might drag on for three years. What with that, the leg, the kids making their own way, the timing seems about right. You're young enough to do more with your life than nurse a declining husband. I hope you'll sell up and go and live near Mary. You're happier with that kind of climate than I am. The sun I'm sitting in at this moment is just my cupper.

Explain to the children, won't you? They may think I've chickened out, but they'll understand in time. I don't want them to feel this decision has all that much to do with us not hitting it off as well as we might, because it hasn't. Most marriages are a compromise, and I don't think you and I have made too bad a job of it, all things considered. Think about taking up again with Bob Sullivan. You've known him longer than you've known me, after all. Now his wife's snuffed it you'll be in the same boat. He's probably not a bad chap when you get to know him!

A movement on the fringe of the wood disturbed his concentration. It was a deer grazing in short grass. A veil of gossamer drifted slowly over the turf across the blue sky, like a backdrop, the long filaments shimmering in the sunlight. Some of the silken threads had hung themselves on a yellow-leafed field maple a few dozen yards to the east. Behind the maple a tall holly, its branches heavy with red berries, still glistened with held pockets of the night's rain. For a few moments he was mesmerized by the beauty of the scene, then he moved the paper, and the deer bounded silently back into the forest, her ears pricked with instant alarm.

It's so lovely up here. A sudden St Martin's

86

Summer. I know you don't get quite the same kick out of the countryside, but I hope you can understand my wanting to peg out while I can still enjoy it. Selfish, I suppose, but there's no point in my being a drain on you and the kids just so that I can grow old ungracefully. Coming to a halt up here makes sense somehow, though my apologies to whoever has to fish me out. I feel bad about leaving you to cope, but I'd have been the first to go anyway and this is less messy. Anyhow, I'm starting to justify myself, so I'd best pack it in and get down to the practicalities.

His attention was distracted again, this time by a brace of pheasants emerging from behind a low bush on the edge of the turf where the ground was spongy with moss and humus and the grass thin below the trees. The birds were engrossed in each other, the cock attentive, the hen receptive, vocally communicating with low notes like those of doves, but harsher. They circled each other, pecking at the ground and billing, then as though their feelings had got the better of them they retired to the privacy of a hollow in the flat-topped bush and billed and cooed and rubbed up against each other in a way he had never before seen in pheasants.

He could tell by sound more than sight that the birds were too immersed in each other to be alarmed by his slight movements. He wondered at the intensity of their feelings when it was not even the mating season. Pheasants had always seemed so stupid, making such a shindy as they flew in dead straight lines, their brief existence dependent upon the strange passion of some well-fed stockbroker to bring them to hard earth in a bumping flurry of soft feathers. It was easy to forget that even at that level of life there could be dependence and communication, a kind of joy.

He tried to finish his letter, but the ending eluded him.

His watch told him an hour had passed. He had better get on with the day's business. He looked at the gin bottle without interest. Neither time nor place seemed right for getting sozzled. His perceptions were sharp, in harmony with his surroundings. But it was the classic method, favoured by most medical men who took their own lives, so as that was why he was there . . .

He unscrewed the cap and took a mouthful of the contents, glad he had diluted it with tonic water. Now, maybe, the right conclusion for his letter would come to him.

Suddenly the pheasants squawked and ran from under the bush, their legs going at comic speed before they took off heavily down hill. For a moment he was worried that someone was approaching, for he had made no particularly sharp movement that might have frightened them. Then he saw the reason for their panic.

"What the devil!" he exclaimed. "Roddy!"

The dog, the pheasants' scent forgotten, raced over to him and went through the full reunion routine. He fondled the animal's head fiercely, half in anger, half gladly.

"You rascal!" he said. "You got out. How the hell did you know where I was?"

Roddy sat beside him, panting. He guessed the dog had covered a lot of ground before picking up his scent. Over the years they had taken many of the wide choice of footpaths.

"You old blighter," he said gruffly. He felt the dog's neck. "You haven't even got a collar. You could have got yourself shot. Some keepers only want an excuse."

He breathed deeply, feeling sudden need to muster resolution. His nostrils felt the pungent, long-loved scent of rotting oak leaves, one of the compensations for each dying year, though now a little in competition with the aftermath of gin.

"This won't do," he said. "You've got to go home."

He imagined his body and that of the dog being found together days, even weeks, later, then told himself to stop sentimentalizing. Hunger would drive the animal home. He lay back in the chair, his hand resting on the dog's back, trying to focus his mind on essentials. A thing worth doing was worth doing well. The adage had governed so much of his life.

He picked up the smaller bottle, giving it a quick, pointless shake. All present and correct. Fifteen 100 mg capsules of pentobarbitone plus five for good measure . . .

Christ! He'd forgotten to take the travel-sickness pill. Charles had advised one an hour before the capsules. "Less chance of bringing them up." Right, no more mucking . . .

He swallowed the pill without taking more gin, in case the combination put him into only temporary sleep. Bloody hell, was he so feeble-minded he couldn't even remember the precaution he had known about from the day he sought his brother's advice? Good old Charles! None of that rubbish about the Hippocratic oath. Blood was thicker when it came to the crunch. "A small breakfast, Toby. Something bland. Porridge would be fine. Calms the stomach without delaying absorption. And dilute the gin; it'll reduce the chance of nausea . . . "

It had been the business of using a plastic bag that had put him off a bit. There was something incongruous, undignified, almost irreverent, about being found in such an idyllic spot with a bin liner over one's head. All right, combined with the sedatives it made the result more certain, but somehow it seemed to be trying too hard. Rather like setting the spinnaker in a steady breeze with only half a mile to go to the finishing line, and the next boat four hundred yards behind. But the aesthetic objection was the strongest. He smiled, remembering the indignant if possibly apocryphal summing-up of that environmentally-sensitive judge: "You have been found guilty of indulging in unnatural practices below one of

89

London's most *beautiful* bridges." There was a parallel.

Roddy had tired of communion and was zig-zagging along the margin of the open ground, snuffling happily at evidence of a world beyond human perception. He had been a wonderful companion, the real instigator of twelve years of regular walking. He tried to suppress the thought that he was as sorry to say good-bye to Roddy as to Sylvia.

But now the dog was saying "come on," not "good-bye." The walk needed completion, in company.

"Sorry, boy. No walkies."

He patted the dog's head. Instead of whining, his usual reaction to unreasonable procrastination, Roddy sat resignedly by the chair, looking contentedly out across the grassy slope to the distant shining sea.

> Roddy's joined me. I hope he'll have the sense to go home when he sees I'm not coming. It may be cheek to ask this in the circumstances, but please don't let him miss his exercise. The paperboy might take him when he walks his mother's dog. They're both labradors.

Again his attention wandered. A large bird was soaring in wide slow spirals over the hill, its tail expanded, the broad rounded wings not moving in relation to its body. Because it was in silhouette against the bright sky, he could not see the colouring, but he knew it was a buzzard. Not a rare bird, of course, but uncommon enough on the Downs to awaken that slight flicker of excitement he had first known as a boy when no prospect made term more endurable than that of spending the weeks' freedom with binoculars and camera on the Dales of his childhood.

Roddy was lying down now, his head resting on his front paws, his eyes fixed on the horizon. It was out of character. He was a push-on dog, disinclined to waste good scent-pursuing minutes taking time out for little rests by the wayside. It was Roddy's seemingly inexhaustible demands that of late had made it increasingly difficult to exercise him. A game leg needs a break every now and then, and Roddy was for total commitment.

"All right, boy?" He put his hand on the dog's haunch.

The animal sighed, got up, turned round twice, then resettled, facing him, eyes meeting his.

He tried to marshal his thoughts:

> Don't forget to reset the thermostat on the boiler when it turns colder. It saves oil. There's a lot of sludge in the tube-gauge by the tank. This may affect the reading next time it's filled. Ask the tanker driver if he'll clear it for you. It's only a question of easing a couple of screws on the clamp and pouring out the muck. I've cleared the gutters of leaves and there shouldn't be many more this year. In future, best get George to see to them. And he'll have to take over the pruning. You'd better lend him my R.H.S. leaflet on the care of fruit trees.

His eyes were feeling heavy. Sun, sickness pill, gin . . . He shook his head. He was so warm in the sun that he pulled the knot of his tie and undid the top button of his shirt. A great peace threatened his determination . . .

When he looked at his watch he realized he had slept for over an hour. The sky was still cloudless, but he felt slightly chilled, though the breeze revealed by the tops of the encircling trees did not reach him in the warm hollow. Roddy had not moved, though his eyes were closed.

"You're making a balls-up of this," he muttered.

He shivered and wrapped the free ends of the rug round him. His letter dropped on to the dog's paws, waking him.

He couldn't even finish the bloody letter, let alone . . .

> I've left a list of things in my desk, including a full statement of the financial position. You shouldn't

> have any worries on that score. The insurance
> won't be affected, by the way . . .

Charles had said take the sickness pill an hour before-
hand. It was now over an hour. He had better get on with
it.

> So there we are, old girl. Sorry again about any
> initial shock, but I think you'll feel it was for the
> best in the long run. It's become a damned stupid
> world and believe me I am less sorry to say good-
> bye to it than to you and Roddy. All my love, Toby.

It wasn't much of an ending, and perhaps he should have
left out Roddy, but best to let it come naturally.

The dog had stood up and stretched and was now sitting
on his haunches regarding him, making none of his usual
attempts to purge idleness by action.

He picked up the small bottle again and unscrewed the
top, tipping its contents on to the palm of his left hand.
He counted each capsule slowly. Twenty exactly.

Roddy sniffed hopefully and licked his chops. The
charm of confectionary had never been lost on him. His
favourites, "love bombs" from the village shop, were
a similar shape to the capsules, though more brightly
coloured, and were also kept in a small bottle. An
unsuitable passion for a doctored labrador.

"Not for you, old boy."

He took a little more gin. He would have preferred a
sandwich; it was well past mid-day. Well, this was it, then.

He poured the capsules back into the bottle, then
tipped two out into his palm. One swig to each pair and
that would be that.

The dog whimpered, his eyes still fixed on him, but
instead of rushing off in his usual heavy, hint-dropping
way, he just sat there, staring.

"Go on," he said, "go find a pheasant."

92

Roddy thumped his tail on the moss-padded ground but made no further move.

"Go *on*," he urged, "go find something."

A squirrel was spiralling up a beech bole, claws audibly scratching the smooth bark, bright eyes alert for life's wide repertoire of perils. The labrador mildly enjoyed getting a rise out of tree-rats, as George called them, but this one he ignored. He lay down again, his eyes still on the man's.

Daft animal! Why did one get so damnably attached to them? He knew why, and it had everything to do with what animals were and humans are not. Sylvia had thought it absurd that a year or more ago, before he had even laid plans for his own exit, he had decided how Roddy was to be put down. Now he would not be able to supervise this. Still, Sylvia knew he wanted it done humanely, at home. If nothing else got him first, of course – such as a lorry if left to find his own way back . . .

He expelled breath between clenched teeth, in resigned irritation, feeling guilt; not because of the mythical lorry so much as because the parallel in their ages had come home to him. The animal was twelve, nearly thirteen. In his eighties if you went along with that seven to one idea. Older than himself.

"Bloody hell!" he said aloud. He was still holding the two capsules in his palm and they were getting sticky. He wasn't winning.

The thought of anti-climax prompted a moment of inner panic. After all that forward planning, all that heart-searching . . . He shot the capsules into his mouth, helping them down with a nip of the gin.

Roddy whimpered, but not with the accompanying business that he laid on when wanting a walk.

"Damn you," he said, "bugger off home."

The dog moved nearer, butting gently at his hand. He guessed his momentary panic had been sensed. He patted Roddy's head, then left his hand there, and the dog closed

93

his eyes, content.

The mid-day sun was almost too much. He lay back in the chair, the drug bottle in one hand, remembering some of the animal's proofs of intelligence and empathy. They were private memories. It was all too easy to be charged with reading too much into an animal's behaviour. Even Sylvia, though reasonably fond of Roddy, had little patience with what she called anthropomorphizing. Her training had been in biology. God, it seemed mean leaving the poor bloody animal behind. Would Sylvia even bother to get the paper-boy to walk him? He still had so much go in him, for all his twelve years.

He fought conscience, but in the quiet beauty of his surroundings his mind worked with disturbing clarity. He argued against the self-judgment of disloyalty to this sloppy four-legged creature in whose company he had spent the happiest hours for years past. But a stronger voice was telling him that a better order of play would have been to see the dog's natural life out before he took his own. A couple of years, if he made it that long, and he would have no obligation.

The sun had brought the sweat out on his forehead. The blue of the sky almost hurt his eyes. He shut them, and a few moments later his right hand slipped from the dog's warm head; his left relaxed, allowing the bottle to tilt and spill its contents on to his lap. Some of the capsules rolled off on to the brown compacted carpet of dead moss and leaf-mould. They glinted invitingly there in the warm sun, not unlike harmless "love bombs". In the impenetrable tangle of bramble bush on the forest's edge a cock pheasant churred and chukkered to its mate, at peace with a world visibly and audibly at peace.

# Trees in Young Green Leaf

F EW YOUNG men could have resisted encouragement from such a beautiful woman – not in Paris, in the spring, with the sap rising. Who was I to martyr myself?

It is unlikely we would have met but for the Marquis de St. Douceur. Who, you may wonder, was the Marquis de St. Douceur? The answer is a shade prosaic. He was the millionaire son of a Wall Street banker. Some might hold that no millionaire can be entirely prosaic, not even from Wall Street. They would be wrong. Left to himself, Goodland Reinhardt – for that was his real name – was as prosaic as they come.

He was a quiet, gentle, retiring, soft-spoken, slow-gesturing little man who dressed summer and winter in pale grey suits with a silky sheen. Few men were more capable of melting into the wallpaper in any gathering exceeding two. The only give-away, the only hint that he was not some small-town office clerk, lay in his eyes. When they met your own you saw that they were a clear and steely blue, the reflection of a mind determined to cherish the source of its owner's strength. Like all multi-millionaires who have stayed that way, Goody had never in his life spent a dime without forethought; and usually not then.

Left to himself, I said. But millionaires seldom are. Society still holds women who favour means other than political and intellectual for achieving liberation. The Baroness Alexandra Naryshkina-Miloslavsky-Romanov, whom Goody had met at the tables in Monte, was a memorable example. Her dazzling if chequered life having underlined the fact that neither pedigree nor culture necessarily pays bills, she had homed in on Goody with a single-mindedness from which he had not the slightest hope of escape.

Not that he wished to escape. Like me, like a thousand other men, Goody was Alexandra's willing slave from the moment they met. She was everything that he was not. She was witty, immoral, extroverted, calculating, absurdly beautiful, and with more energy and determination than anyone he had known or imagined. She knew everyone who mattered and had an unerring instinct for those who didn't. She charmed all men, infuriated most women, but was ignored by neither. She knew how, when, where and why to behave properly, and under what circumstances to behave thoroughly badly, such as in bed where she introduced Goody to dimensions beyond his wildest dreams. She also knew how to spend money, which Goody, who lacked this faculty, not only admired but, strangely, encouraged. But because she did not much fancy being restricted by the name of Mrs Goodland Reinhardt, on the eve of marriage she consulted an old friend, the aunt of a European prince and the last subsiding member of the St. Douceur family. For a modest consideration in seven figures – francs, I grant you – the prince's aunt legally adopted Goody and had the title Marquis de St. Douceur conferred upon him. These things are easily arranged when one knows the ropes.

But I stray from the point, which is that now Goody has died, six years after Alexandra, lonely and inconsolable in his Palm Beach condominium, I have been thinking back to when I stayed with them in Paris, that painful span of years ago.

They had a flat there, an apartment larger than most houses, in the Avenue Henri-Martin. The salon was immensely high with pillared, mirrored walls, much gilt, and exquisitely painted ceilings. From an ante-room came vociferous evidence of a free-ranging colony of parrots, parakeets and mynah birds, and while I sat in the salon listening to this unorchestrated cacophony I refreshed myself from the tray of figs, apples and lemon-laced spring water provided by the white-coated houseman who had let me in.

My chair was ornate – Louis the something-or-other, no doubt – and I remember crossing my legs, feeling potentially worldly but actually apprehensive, my heart fluttering at the prospect of meeting for only the second time the delectable Alexandra. That in years she could have been my own mother was neither here nor there.

It puzzled me, I recall, that the Reinhardts should have invited me to stay, albeit that it was only for a single night. Like most of the rich, they shared with the theatrical profession an intense appetite for being remembered. To achieve this immortality for as long as possible, it is good policy to impinge upon the memory of the young. Why else would they have bothered with someone so unsophisticated and tender as myself?

Mind you, Goody had for years been a fervent admirer of my mother who in her way had acquired as loyal a following as Alexandra, though in her reclusiveness and pursuit of ideas she was as different as chalk from cheese. And because she had long refused to see or be seen by anyone except me, I was uniquely qualified to bring Goody up to date on matters my mother would not have considered worth mentioning in her letters to him. Not that I had much to report except that she was still devoting every wakeful hour to writing books that continued to attract their intensely enthusiastic but numerically insignificant readership.

Their point of contact was a shared desire to make the world a kinder place for animals. In Goody's case this was the beginning and the end of his idealism. In my mother's, it was part of a wider philosophy. Self-taught, this was in

97

the Platonic tradition. She held that society could be no better than the people it contained, and that only a universal return to belief in the Supreme Good could save the sinking ship of Western civilisation. With hindsight, and taking a level look at Western civilisation, I suspect she had it about right.

But although Goody subscribed to her conviction, he lacked the concentration to think it through. Like me, he was happy to stay with the bit that related to the animals. My mother, who with the time saved by not meeting people wrote letters of great length and persuasion, rebuked him for this limited field of vision. He accepted her rebukes – indeed, he positively invited them – and confirmed in letters of equal enthusiasm if less literary merit his agreement that only an embracing of the Supreme Good was going to get anywhere at all.

What helped to keep the correspondence going was the difference between my mother's outlook and Goody's; while she held that no particular action needed to be taken to this end apart from pressing into the hands of every man, woman and child a copy of her last three books, Goody had the more masculine but possibly less realistic belief that change would be effected through institutions and the power of political systems. My mother had little patience with such woolly wishful thinking. When, from time to time, she was provoked to concentrated demolition of his naive proposition, Goody would not attempt verbal defence. Instead, he would send her snapshots of the lama, the python, the Siberian tiger, the black swans, and the other exotica he and Alexandra kept in a private safari park in the grounds of their castle in Spain.

This would annoy my mother intensely, because she was concerned with the spiritual evolution of Goody and the animals, not with pictures of either, and his non-violent posting of batches of en-prints was clear evasion of the issue. "Douceurs!" she would say contemptuously, casting them into the bin by her desk. So he got back even more severe letters, which pleased him enormously. He kept them in a stout box file and read most of them many times for sheer intellectual stimulation, often in bed with Alexandra before the light went out. I did not see it then, but I suppose Alexandra and my mother catered in their separate ways for the body and mind of Goody, a body and mind ripe for the solace of domination.

Be that as it may, in the matter of making the lives of non-human species more endurable there was genuine *rapport*, and that is why I was standing in the Bois where, in her unbelievable fifties, Alexandra rode twice daily, gazing at the bust of the horse. The hunk of rock on which it was set had been inscribed:

Étalon Amiral
Champion de la race Morgan
offert au
Bois de Boulogne
par
Goodland Reinhardt, Marquis de St. Douceur

That this beautiful girl was already contemplating the bust when I came upon it was an entirely fortuitous bonus on a glorious spring day in Paris.

The technique for making the acquaintance of pretty women comes more readily in youth than later in life. Or it did, within reason, for me. In this case, the circumstances made technique almost unnecessary. For a few seconds I stood within two feet of her, a little behind and to one side. She had a deliciously delicate profile, and in the curve of her sharply defined lips I thought I detected the hint of a smile. Her dark hair was held away from her face, a comb and God knew what other small devices retaining its bulk above the nape of her graceful neck. Strangely, to this day I remember her neck more clearly than her face. It was long and slim, eminently for display, its skin so white and soft that the temptation to stroke it was almost irresistible. I longed for her to turn her head, to see it pivot on its enchanting column, to gaze upon her face in its entirety.

"Très curieux, n'est-ce pas?" I ventured.

As was doubtless clear to her, my command of the French language had made little progress since I left school. She turned her head, smiled faintly, and answered me in those broken accents that alone do so much to make French women attractive to Englishmen of any age.

"Curieux? I do not see why."

I stammered, already head over heels in calf-love with the exquisite, cat-like, doe-eyed features on which I gazed:

"To erect a monument to a horse."

She shrugged. "It is done all the time, is it not? In every great city there are statues of men and horses."

"But usually," I argued weakly, relieved by her willingness to talk to me, "the horse carries a man. It is rare to see the horse alone, and commemorated by a private individual."

"This Marquis," she said, "was very attached to the creature to have paid for such a luxury."

I was young, she was beautiful. She was also, I had realised, a few years older than myself. The temptation to arouse her interest in me was overwhelming.

"In fact," I said, "the attachment was between the horse and the wife."

"Vraimant!" she said with an amused pull of the mouth. "I see why you use the word 'curious'."

"I don't mean like that," I said hastily. "Merely that the Marquis's wife was the horse-rider."

"So you know the family?"

"They are friends of my mother," I admitted. "But, yes, I do know them. I am staying in their apartment."

"The rich are rather sad," she said. "They go to such lengths to achieve immortality."

"The Reinhardts are not sad. They lead very full lives

100

and are devoted to each other."

"And how do they fill those lives?" she asked, as without spoken agreement we began to walk together.

I told her all I knew about the Reinhardts as we strolled slowly through the Bois in the warm sunshine, through trees in young green leaf.

Her name was Martine. Below a rose-pink velvet jacket carried loosely over her shoulders, she wore a floral dress of some very delicate material, browns and pinks predominating, so light that I suspected the laced hem to be a necessary precaution against the breeze. Years were to pass before the drab, ubiquitous jeans became the uniform of the young. She had a small waist, banded by a thin gold belt, and her brown high-heeled shoes held a strand of the same colour. I wished that I did not have to return to England the next day.

"But you have not really answered my question," she said – "as to how they spend their lives."

"The animals and birds need constant attention. Not only here, but on their estate in Spain."

She nodded. "It is a common distraction. People can become the slaves of animals."

"But they are devoted to them," I protested. "Alexandra perhaps more than Goody. It was she who first opened Goody's eyes to the part they could play in relieving animal suffering. They rescued many from appalling cruelty, particularly in Spain."

"Yes," she said, "we are a cruel race." She shrugged. "It is how we are. You cannot change human nature."

"But human nature is not consistent," I said. "There are people who are not cruel. There are those who have never wished to cause suffering – not to animals, anyway. If we were all cruel, there could be no exceptions."

"Our natures are complicated. We do not share the same priorities. Those who love animals often hate humans."

"Perhaps with reason," I said. "I think if I saw a hunter

101

about to kill a gorilla in order to take her young, only the thought of punishment would restrain me from killing him first."

"The English are so sentimental," she said with a smile. "It is very charming."

Her face had lost some of its beauty.

"I don't call that sentiment," I objected. "It is cause and effect. There is something in us – you see it in children before they accept their parents' values – that sympathises and wants to protect. Such instincts are educated out of us by the society we are born into."

"You are a strange boy," she said. "You seem to have thought much about these things."

"It's a matter of observation," I said. "I suppose I was brought up to think for myself."

"Ah, well," she said, shaking her head, "does anyone really do that?"

She asked about my background and interests, and I was soon back in love with her. We talked of other things – of films, of books, of art and music, of the way the world was going, of all that at that stage of life is fresh and important. I wanted to prolong our time together. She was doing nothing in particular.

"Might we have lunch together?" I said.

We left the Bois by the Porte Maillot, where I insisted we take a taxi to Fouquets in the Champs Elysees. We drank coffees there, at idiotic cost, and she assured me she was not hungry enough for lunch.

"Shall we go to the Sacre Coeur and look out over Paris?" she suggested. "Then we could visit a few galleries in the Louvre and have a little something to eat on the other side of the river."

It was basic tourism, budget-style, but I loved her the more for suggesting what would not take me out of my depth, culturally or financially.

"I wish you could come back to the Reinhardts," I said as we left the Louvre, "but it would be a little difficult.

102

They are not expecting me until this evening."

We crossed the Pont des Arts and ate in the self-service Latin-Cluny on the corner of the rue de la Harpe and the Boulevard St. Germain. If not the peak of intimacy and haute-cuisine, the Latin-Cluny was so thronged with students that I felt relaxed and happy and further under the spell of Martine. The evening staying warm, she needed only to slip her little pink jacket over her bare arms when, after our meal, we walked back to the Seine and strolled round the Ile de la Cité. A cool breeze swept over the water and Martine shivered – reason enough to put my arm across her shoulders and suggest we seek the warmth of a café.

We made our way past the Sorbonne and the Pantheon to a small café in the Place Contrescarpe where we sat at a table in the shadowed corner of the warm room. It was the sort of place only students and Parisians would have known about, not in the least touristy. In the warmth, over the small round table, proximity bred boldness in me, encouraged by Martine who sent the blood pumping through my body with sudden intimate pressures on my arms and hands. Charming, flirtatious, she was, as I realised later, leaving me something to remember her by. It was one of those moments that the passing years enshrine in sentiment, as still as a bee in amber.

"And now," she said, suddenly practical, pulling on her little jacket, "I regret, but I must go home. Shall we share a taxi to the Boulevard Haussmann, then it can take you on to your friends?"

She so clearly intended that that was what should happen that I attempted no romantic overtures. Just how I might have contrived to spend the night in Martine's arms had become a very real preoccupation, but experience and the francs in my wallet left her to do the running.

In the taxi we sat in opposite corners and returned to discussing the Reinhardts.

"The cooling-off period," I remarked, the bolder for knowing I was in no delicious danger. "You are très pratique!"

She smiled and touched my hand, but with friendship rather than intimacy.

"I have enjoyed our day together," she said.

The taxi had stopped.

"I do not even know your other name," I protested.

She shrugged. "Charron. Have a good journey tomorrow."

"I may decide to stay on," I said desperately. But the door had already closed. With a smile and a wave she dismissed me and the taxi, and as it pulled away from the kerb I just had time to note the number on the wall of the house.

The Reinhardts returned five minutes after I got in.

"Darling, you are here already," Alexandra said, peeling long gloves off fingers laden with rings representing several fortunes. "Have you been in long? Are you desperately bored? How frightful of us not to be back to greet you."

"Not at all," I said. "I've just this moment arrived."

"My God!" Alexandra said. "What an evening! How dull it has been. Goody, my darling, pour me a vodka."

"I found your statue in the Bois," I said.

"Statue? Of my darling Amiral! Ah, what a horse that was! But my true love, my greatest, was Le Cid. Did I tell you about him? He was a magnificent white stallion. We saw him in a film, a very famous film, and I said to Goody, 'That horse, my darling, is all that I want in the whole world.' Of course, I did not really mean it, but . . . " She shrugged. "Then two weeks later, when I had forgotten the film and we were back in Spain, my darling stallion was waiting for me, saddled and ready, when I went to the stables one morning."

Goody nodded, handing Alexandra her drink. "She got right on him," he said, "and off they galloped across the

104

hills as though they had been doing it for ever. They didn't come back until it was dark. I was sweating blood."

"It was love at first sight," Alexandra said. "Never, before or since, have I felt about a horse as I felt about Le Cid."

"I am sorry you have been bored this evening," I said. "Was it a dull play?"

"A play? No, my darling, we have not been to the theatre. It was a dinner. Goody is the President of the International Union for the Protection of Animals. There were speeches. When these affairs are international, so many people have to make speeches. No country can be overlooked or there are – feelings. It was interminable."

"I tried to keep them short," Goody murmured. "But it was a big occasion for them, honey."

"I know, darling, I know. It was one of those things where one has to set the teeth. To grin and bear it. Marcus knows what I mean, don't you, Marcus? There are times when one must be very stoical and British."

"You will never be anything so dull," I said, suddenly fearful that it might sound rude.

Alexandra laughed. Parted lips are so often the older woman's give-away, but Alexandra's smile and laughter were enchanting. Her teeth might have been those of a girl half her age. Her skin was as smooth and delectable as Martine's.

"A few hours in Paris," she said, "and you are already a *galant!*"

I am horribly afraid that at that point I blushed.

My dreams that night were confused, nightmarish, featuring Alexandra and Martine in roles that brought me nothing but frustration and fear. I woke again and again, each time convinced I was going out of my mind. By dawn my bed was soaked with perspiration.

The houseman brought my breakfast. Alexandra rose very late when they stayed in Paris, so I scribbled a thank-

105

you, and left the apartment soon after ten. My luggage was a light grip, so I walked straight to the Boulevard Haussmann and found Martine's door. The blue and white number set in the stone had recurred in my dreams. If the night's disquiet had produced any resolution, it was to see Martine again.

It was another apartment block. In the hallway was a discrete row of name-boards. One of them read:

JEAN-PAUL CHARRON : CHIRURGIEN
ESTHÉTIQUE

"Esthétique" was within my reach, but "chirurgien" needed my pocket dictionary. She had not told me that her father was a plastic-surgeon, but there was so much I had not asked.

Apartment five was on the first floor. I rang the bell, my mind trying to sort out the options for when a nurse or receptionist asked my business. But Martine opened the door.

"Hullo!" she said, smiling but not noticeably surprised.

"I . . . I just had to see you," I said, relying upon honesty.

"Then you had better come in."

She led me across the hall and through double doors. The salon was bright, warm, full of sun from the long windows, the pastel furnishings expensive and in good taste. Low couches, a love-seat, big table lamps and bowls of fresh flowers gave a feeling of luxurious relaxation. A grand-piano bore a dozen or more framed photographs.

"May I offer you some coffee?" she said, quite formally, as though I were a patient awaiting her father's attentions.

"Thank you, that would be terrific."

I sat on one of the couches and flipped through a glossy fashion magazine. Like everything in the room, it had style, sophistication. My heart was thumping and I felt

106

like a newly-taught swimmer who, wading out to deeper water, is having to walk on his toes to keep contact with the sand.

Martine brought in the coffee, steaming, fragrant, as only the French seem capable of making it. Small, sweet biscuits were prettily arranged on a charming flowered plate. Martine sat on the love-seat. Its only other occupant was a toy seal with a face as irresistible in its way as Martine's.

"This is a pleasant surprise," she said demurely.

"I'm sorry," I said, not really knowing what I meant; but Martine seemed to understand.

"It is a shame you have to leave today," she said.

I took my courage in both hands. "I don't absolutely have to," I said. "I could stay on a day or two if . . . if there was reason."

She offered me a biscuit. "You have reasons?"

I bit on the biscuit. The crumbs caught in my throat, so I had to gulp some coffee.

"I'd . . . I'd like to have reasons," I admitted.

I rose and walked toward the window, needing some form of activity to cover my gaucherie, my hateful lack of poise. For the first time in my life I ached to be ten years older. I looked down on the wide street, its trees in new leaf: Paris in the spring; a lovely girl in a warm room; a full heart, and a mind in hopeless panic. It was one hell of a mixed blessing to be young.

"Would you like another coffee?" Martine enquired.

I walked to the next tall window, then turned back into the room, knowing I had to face it out. As I passed the grand piano I saw a photograph of Alexandra. It stopped me in my tracks. I read the large tempestuous inscription in the lower right hand corner: "To Jean-Paul – saint and saviour. For always. Alexandra, Marquise de St. Douceur."

She was seated on an ornate white bench below a pair of huge iron-studded doors. Sharing the bench, its chin resting adoringly in Alexandra's outstretched hand, was a shining, sleek puma. At her feet lay a dog of massive proportions, a thick leather thong connecting its wide decorated collar to Alexandra's slim wrist. Her enormous ostrich-feathered picture hat matched the white satin of her long dress, below which small red shoes peeped demurely. If the jewels round her neck were all they looked, they would have bought a continent.

"The Pope married them," Martine said. "Those are the doors of their private chapel in Spain. I believe the marriage cost them a lot of money."

"You didn't tell me," I said.

"That we know the Reinhardts?" She smiled. "No, we never seemed to get round to it."

"But you should have said," I rebuked. "You let me run on about them."

She shrugged. "It does not matter. It was a little game. Anyway, they are more my father's friends than mine."

"The inscription," I said " – 'saviour'?"

"Alexandra was a patient."

"But a chirurgien esthétique is a specialist. As we say, a plastic surgeon."

"Exactly. Alexandra was one of plastic surgery's big successes."

"But why? Some accident? Her riding?"

Martine laughed. "No, no, nothing like that. She simply . . . well, wanted her face attended to."

"I don't understand. If she had had no accident . . ."

She laughed again. "Women do not have to have accidents in order to seek surgery. Alexandra just felt there was room for improvement."

"You mean she had a face-lift."

"A little more than that."

I was curious. "More?"

Martine nodded. "If you will promise not to tell anyone at all, least of all the Reinhardts, I think I can show you something that will make you understand."

"I shan't tell a soul."

She poured me some more coffee and left the room. I moved back to the piano and studied Alexandra's photograph. She was unbelievably lovely, but the ostrich feather worried me. I had read about ostrich farms. Martine returned, carrying a large envelope.

"These will explain," she said.

We sat on the low couch, side by side. Until then I had never realised that perfume could be so erotic. I wanted to take her in my arms, to force myself upon her, with or against her will. The photograph Martine withdrew from the envelope cooled my ardour. It showed the face of a distinctly middle-aged woman. She had heavy eyes, a rather ugly nose, and a mouth that not merely lacked beauty but strongly hinted of malice, even cruelty. Her jowl was heavy and her neck no longer firm.

"Who . . . ?" I began, already knowing the answer.

Martine nodded. "Alexandra . . . how do you say? Before."

"I can't believe it," I said.

"Few things are what they seem," Martine replied. "But, yes, it was an exceptional transformation. Without her personality, her determination, it would not have been so successful. When a woman truly desires change, you know, she puts all her heart and mind into it."

I had an illogical feeling of having been deceived.

"Well at least there has been no change in her love of animals," I said.

"Love? It depends what one means by such words. I think there are people, like yourself perhaps, who really have . . . what is the word? . . . sympathy. Who feel another's hurt. Who . . . "

"Identify?"

"I think so. But something more than a rapport. Such people are rare. I do not believe Alexandra is one of them."

"They why else . . . ?"

"She had four husbands before Goody, you know, but

109

never any children. There is so much energy there, so much emotion needing a target."

"I see what you're saying, but it seems inadequate, cynical."

Martine put the envelope down on the love-seat and picked up the toy seal. She stroked it fondly.

"This is my Pho-Pho. He is beautiful, is he not?"

I fondled the creature's head and began to stroke its fur. Our hands touched, and once again Martine's perfume asserted itself.

"It is so realistic," I said. "Almost like a real animal."

"But, yes," Martine said, her voice light but matter-of-fact, "that is exactly what it is. A real baby seal. How do you say? L'empaillage? Filled?"

I withdrew my hand. "Stuffed? A real seal?"

Martine nodded. "Very pretty, yes?"

The perfume had become a mere smell, the room less light and warm. My stomach seemed to have sunk several inches.

"I . . . I don't understand," I said, "how you could want a real seal to be killed to make you a toy."

"Oh, but it was years ago. Besides, it was a present. From Alexandra."

"But Alexandra wouldn't . . ."

"She is very impulsive. Very warm. There was an accident – to me, you understand. The Reinhardts had friends with a big estate at Fontainebleau. My parents knew them well. Aristocrats. Sometimes they invited Alexandra to hunt with them . . ."

"Alexandra?" I interrupted. "Hunt?"

Martine, her head a little on one side, regarded me quizzically.

"You are a little in love with her, yes?"

I shrugged. The gesture was non-committal but I could feel the colour flooding my face.

"I just can't imagine Alexandra killing anything – for fun."

110

"You must relax more, Marcus," Martine said. "Try to be more . . . gay. To be too sensitive is to be too easily hurt." Her matter-of-factness returned. "Anyway, Alexandra was bound to receive such invitations. She was such a magnificent horsewoman. She still it. Because I ride a little, I was invited too, and that day I fell and hurt myself quite badly. Almost enough . . ." she laughed ". . . to need my husband's attention."

"Your husband?"

"Yes, he is the surgeon. Did you not realise?"

"You said . . ." I stopped, aware that I had assumed, not been told. Martine had asked so much about myself.

"Anyway," she went on, "Alexandra sent me Pho-Pho to cheer me up when my neck was in a collar. The picture over the bureau shows me just before the accident. I was wearing a little hunting cap. Très chic, n'est ce pas?"

I had no wish to gaze upon Martine in her little hunting cap. I felt slightly sick. I had seen all I wanted to see of Paris in the spring.

"I have a 'plane to catch," I said. "The coffee was very nice."

Apologies. This has not made much of a story. More an episode, an encapsulation, and at times perhaps a shade too close for comfort to the women's magazines. But sometimes life is like that, don't you think? To falsify for the sake of literary purity, to sustain a style, is unacceptable.

Maybe apology is not appropriate, for if the end is disappointing – as, indeed, it was for me those many years ago – it is at least nearer to truth than the contrivances of fiction.

If you should be in Paris one day, with time to spare and near the Bois, seek out the bust of Amiral. It is there, I assure you.

And who knows? In Paris, in the spring, when the sap is rising . . .

111

# Pigs are Sensitive

IF IT hadn't been for Georgie, Pig might never have been one of the family.

Georgie, it must be explained, was three fingers manipulated by their owner Tristram Hallison to strut around the table at the children's meal times, first and third fingers serving as legs, the second projecting horizontally as trunk and head combined.

Once into his stride Georgie ceased to be an extension of Tristram's arm and took on a life of his own. He was into everything, bored by nothing, forever probing, criticizing, encouraging and daring to the total delight of the twins.

He was vocal to boot, never at a loss for words. The voice was Tristram's, of course, but it came over high and semi-ventriloquized, and as all eyes were on Georgie rather than on Tristram, every word was unquestioned evidence of its owner's racy, rebellious, mini-Bond slant on life. George did and got away with things that Simon and Emily would not have dreamed of. He even defied parents. He lived dangerously – and survived. He was as much part of the family as Mewlie the cat or the dog Clutterbuck; *persona grata* any time, any place.

Drab to record, he had been invented only to encourage the twins to acquire the strange habit of eating, that instinct so often seemingly absent in the young of *Homo sapiens*. Tristram, to whom fatherhood had come late, found mealtime battles rather a strain. Georgie was born

112

of necessity. Omnivorous as well as omnipotent, he would tackle almost anything that appeared on a plate – with appropriate slurping noises, needless to add – though he was smart enough to have a few pet hates at the very mention of which he would lie on his back (which is to say Tristram's knuckles) with hysterical cries of "Eeeugh!" and "Yeuck!" Fortunately these substances did not include the basic foods.

That was many years ago, however. Georgie never lost favour, but his appearances became less frequent. As the twins grew, teddy bears and dolls took more of the limelight. The most favoured among them also acquired speech and viewpoints that at times slightly alarmed Ann who had studied child psychology for a year before marriage.

"I don't think it matters that you anthropomorphize the toys," she said once, "but you've turned that giraffe into a psychopathic criminal and he's the twins' favourite."

"They'll survive," Tristram had said cheerfully.

They survived quite well. Simon went into engineering without even a passing glance at alternative lifestyles, and a year after her brother left home Emily married a young solicitor whose eligibility was a source of amazement and envy to surrounding parents whose children, deep into their thirties, all seemed to be in competition with each other in the forging of disastrous alliances and hopeless dead-end jobs.

It was Emily who introduced Pig. A kind-hearted girl, she knew that her parents would feel the gap when she married, for until then the free-lance journalism she combined with part-time work for Friends of the Planet had meant that she still saw a lot of home.

And home was where the reception was held, for it was high summer and the gamble they took on the weather had paid off. Everything went well apart from the cake-making woman getting the date wrong, and by three o'clock the car was ready; which was to say it was plastered with lipstick, hung with streamers and old shoes, trailing a string of cans, and properly equipped beneath the bonnet with a kipper on the engine casing.

The last thing Emily did before stepping into the passenger's seat was to hand Ann a small parcel.

"Thank you for everything, mummy," she said. "Daddy, too. This is to keep you company. I couldn't resist him."

They could see why. About eight inches long, Pig was pink, wide, rectangular, stub-legged, flop-eared, and wore a broad engaging grin. The triangular black and white Design Centre label that dangled from his tail gave him a certain panache. Calico-skinned, he was firmly fleshed rather than cuddly, but there was something about him of instant appeal. For a few weeks he was given pride of place on the bureau in the sitting room, next to the carriage clock and within sniffing distance of the flowers Ann kept there.

Then one day she found Pig lying in their bed with the duvet drawn up to his chin so that only his broad grin and the tips of his ears were visible.

"Oh, Tristram!" Ann said, though he wasn't there, golf claiming much of his time since retirement. She removed Pig and put him on Tristram's pillow before doing what she had come into the room to do, which was to put some towels in the drawer. As she was leaving the room she paused and considered for a moment, then picked up Pig and pushed his snout under Tristram's pillow so that only his pink rump was showing, with the Design Centre label hanging from his tail.

From then on there was no telling where Pig would turn up next. He wasn't a talkative animal, in fact he never spoke at all, but he was inquisitive and adventurous to a degree. He was also ambitious and a bit of a worrier. One day Ann found him with his snout deep in an encyclopaedia, intensely studying an article headed "Pigment migration in amphibians."

114

"I see Pig's into literature again," she said.

"Learning more than literature," Tristram replied seriously. "He seems to have worked up rather a worry about his educational deficiencies. I wouldn't be surprised if he starts to agitate for an Open University course before long."

It was all played quite straight, of course. Part of the game.

The months went by. They saw Simon and Emily from time to time, but although they missed them more than either wanted to admit, it went without saying that they had suppressed firmly and responsibly any temptation to drift into possessiveness and interference. The young had their own lives to lead, and that was that.

But a calico pig, however engaging, is no substitute for a meaningful, committed, on-going relationship, and it has to be said that mere suppression of the fact that they missed the children did not make up for their absence. Truth to tell, without mouths to feed, school fees to pay, and with various modest insurance policies reaching maturity, neither Tristram nor Ann had enough to do. Sport and the Women's Institute fill some gaps, but not all. Serving on the golf club committee, and teasing jam pot covers out of rural biddies in the surrounding villages, do not stretch a couple only a little past the prime of life. Books – though there were many around the house – were no longer the draw they used to be. Selectivity over television programmes had not yet been abandoned.

Life's small irritations began to multiply. Perspectives changes. Pig was no longer found daily in some different situation of enquiry or carefree bliss. In fact he spent long intervals neglected by both of them, as often as not haunch-deep in the green flokati rug bought to go between the twin beds it had been decided, for a variety of reasons, were the most sensible replacement for the squashy old double.

When he was remembered, his reanimation was more

likely to be exploited to underline some grievance between Tristram and Ann than to emphasize the free-ranging *joie de vivre* of an exploratory, life-hungry pig. In short, Pig was being manipulated.

His thirst for knowledge was particularly exploited. After an argument, Pig might well be found with his snout buried in some book, his small, intelligent eyes scanning a paragraph that supported one or other side.

This sort of thing is all very well and might have done no harm. If one takes the view that a calico pig is as likely a tool for human catharsis as any other, it is possible to point to positive good in the development. But the situation did not stay static. It progressed. Which is to say it got nastier.

Pig began to be turned upon. Not, let it be clear, by way of physical assault from whip, stick or boot, but – and which may be worse – by ridicule and even open dislike. Trivial things taken singly, no doubt, but cumulatively . . .

In the kitchen, for example. Tristram, like a lot of men who marry late after establishing a workable bachelor routine, was a stickler for cleanliness. Let's put it higher than that: he was bloody fussy. Ann's approach to domestic chores, however, was somewhat slapdash. What is slapdash when all else in marriage is reasonably harmonious can earn less jocular judgments when things deteriorate.

"Do we *have* to live like pigs?" Tristram demanded one lunch-time, rubbing vigorously with a pot scourer at a frying-pan whose encrustations were formidable.

The next day Pig was found by Ann when she entered the kitchen to make breakfast. He was on the dresser looking pointedly at a carving knife whose blade bore evidence of distinctly relaxed washing up.

Ann sighed. She was at her best in the morning, so when Tristram came in she said lightly:

"You shouldn't have let him in the kitchen and shown him the carving knife. The associations are unfortunate.

116

Pigs are sensitive. I read somewhere they sometimes die of fright when being dragged to slaughter."

Tristram was an owl rather than a lark. What was more, a heavy nineteenth hole had been followed by a committee wrangle that had sent him to bed with a splitting headache.

"Oh, for heaven's sake," he said, "isn't it about time we stopped this nonsense? He's only a cloth pig; a lump of inanimate felt."

"*You* brought him into it," Ann said.

For a few days Pig was back on the flokati rug. Ann rather enjoyed waking up to a misty view of a pink pig grinning broadly in a green field of dyed goat's hair.

But matters did not improve. From being cast in partisan roles, Pig was transformed slowly but surely into an animal of independent, gratuitous nastiness. His reading became more and more sociological and liberated. His snout was constantly pressed to purple passages emphasizing the battle of the sexes. Where once he had been wont to peruse amusing and charming thoughts from Alison Uttley and Kenneth Grahame, now he was immersed in the products of Virago, The Women's Press, and authors such as Kingsley Amis, Angus Wilson, Hemingway, and others with even more jaundiced and chauvinistic views of the female sex. He would be found looking at pictures too – pictures of battered wives, men or women murdered by their spouses, even of Playboy women portrayed as sex objects, and of animals hunted, vivisected and otherwise ill-treated by men. The whole thing was becoming very very unpleasant.

One morning Ann came down to make breakfast and discovered Pig on the sofa in the sitting room. Propped in front of him was an encyclopaedia with a luridly coloured illustration of an eviscerated pig hanging from a butcher's hook. The text below read:

In earlier days meat animals were slaughtered by

117

strangulation or by piercing the brain through the eye with heated spears. Blood was left in to cure as an essential part of the meat. Later, the Judaeo-Christian distaste for blood led to new practices: animals were dispatched by a head blow or by severing the jugular vein, the carcass being hung head downward to bleed. After bleeding, cattle and sheep were skinned; pigs were dipped into vats of scalding water so that hair or hide or both could be easily removed.

For whatever reason, Ann felt the colour drain from her face as she snatched the book from before Pig's eyes and slammed it shut on the table. Absurdly, she felt the prick of tears. Tristram came down for breakfast. Ann banged Tristram's coffee cup on to the table and filled it, her hand shaking.

"I don't think that was the least bit funny or called for," she said.

"What wasn't?" Tristram enquired. The weather looked good and a day's golf lay ahead.

"Leaving that . . . disgusting article for Pig to read."

"I don't know what you're talking about."

"Don't be ridiculous, Tristram. Of course you know."

"I tell you I don't."

"He was reading about slaughterhouses in the encyclo-paedia."

"He wasn't reading anything. He's a toy pig."

"He may be a toy, but there is such a thing as bad taste."

"Oh, for heaven's sake!" Tristram said, "Why spoil for a fight on such a lovely day? Look, I really must get on."

Ann opened her mouth, then shut it. Whatever had got into Tristram, she was getting nowhere.

"Well, I'm not amused," she said. "Here's your egg. I'm seeing mother this evening. Have the pork chops."

118

A few days later Ann again found Pig reading, this time in the kitchen with his snout pressed to another page in the encyclopaedia. The article was headed "Hog Slaughter":

> After stunning, pigs are bled by severing one of the large veins, the anterior vena cava, and then submerged in a scalding tank to loosen the hair. After being suspended vertically from a rail and shaved and singed, the carcass is opened with a straight cut in the centre of the belly . . .

Ann was half angry, half worried. Until recently Tristram had at least been subtle in his anthropomorphic fantasies. Even the nastier and getting-at-her inventions of recent weeks had been marked by finesse and humour, however black. The sheer bludgeoning insensitivity of repeating the slaughterhouse joke – if joke was how he had seen it – was out of character.

"Look," she said when he came in, "I do honestly think we have got to stop this Pig thing. What on earth was the point of your latest contrivance?"

She gestured toward the working surface next to the stove where she had left Pig and the propped up book.

It was Tristram's turn to be worried.

"Are you all right?" he enquired.

"I'm very upset."

"But what are you trying to achieve?"

"Achieve?"

"In setting up Pig with that encyclopaedia."

"Me? Don't be absurd. You know perfectly well it is another of your sick ideas of humour or of scoring off me or something."

Tristram attempted a smile of patience and pacification at the same time as a gesture of frustration and impotence.

"Oh, now, look here!" he said. "When we went to bed last night the animal was on the rug. I know because I

119

stepped on him when the bulb went in the table lamp."

"And you took him down with you when you went to get a replacement."

"I didn't."

"Of course you did. You must have."

"I tell you I didn't."

"Then what are you suggesting?"

"Oh, for God's sake," Tristram said, "this is utterly ludicrous. Let's just call a truce and leave it at that."

Things were a little better between them over the next couple of weeks, but on a Sunday morning Ann discovered Pig in the sitting room again, this time snouting through a pamphlet issued by one of the animal-welfare societies. Once again the subject was meat animals, the opened page emphasizing the small proportion of beasts whose slaughter, globally viewed, could be regarded as in any sense humane. It was sober, statistical stuff and called for explanation.

When Tristram had drunk his first cup of coffee and was well into the sausages Ann said:

"Have you been trying to get something through to me all this time?"

"Through to you? What about?"

"I mean, has something made you feel we should go vegetarian?"

Tristram's expression registered surprise, almost shock. "Are you mad?"

"Well, I wouldn't mind too much if you were really set on it. We could take it by degrees."

Tristram put down his knife and fork.

"Would you mind explaining what you are talking about?"

Ann handed him the pamphlet.

"You aren't seriously denying you put that with Pig last night?"

"Of course I'm denying it. I don't think I've ever even

120

seen this pamphlet before."

"It's probably Emily's. She was a junior member of the RSPCA, if you remember."

"So?"

"So it has been on the shelves and you must have found it."

Tristram thumped the table.

"I tell you I haven't seen this bloody leaflet before."

Ann clenched her hands so hard that the nails gave her pain.

"For goodness sake," she pleaded in a voice higher than normal, "will you stop this awful, senseless game? We made a truce."

"The only game I am playing," said Tristram grimly, "is the game of golf, and that is precisely what I shall be doing for the rest of the day. As for that pig, get rid of it. Burn it. Anything."

He flung his napkin on to the table and stamped out of the room, his toast untouched.

Ann wept.

It was the usual thing of the milk bottles. The Hallisons' consumption had long been steady and they were always careful to tell the dairy if they were going to be away.

"The front door's easiest, sarge," P.C. Bates said. "Glass panel right above the Yale."

There was nothing untoward in the hall, nor in the sitting room.

"I'll look upstairs," the sergeant said. "You take the dining room and kitchen."

The main bedroom was untidy and the bed had been slept in, but there was nothing sinister about it. On one pillow, the duvet pulled up under what passed for its chin, was a pink toy pig with a seraphic grin. The sergeant was looking at the photographs on the dressing table when from downstairs came a choked, horrified half scream, half shout. He was down the stairs at good speed for so heavy a man.

The young constable staggered out of the kitchen, bent like an aspen, his hand over his mouth. He was as white as a clown.

The sergeant pushed past him, then stopped abruptly, his large boots inches from the shallow lake of blood that covered the floor. On the table, on the working surfaces, on the chairs, were the visible and stinking signs of unbelievable carnage. A blood-encrusted carving knife lay on the draining board.

"For Christ's sake," the sergeant said thickly when capable of speech, "it's a bloody holocaust."

P.C. Bates, who had brought up in the hall, looked over the sergeant's shoulder.

"They've been butchered," he said weakly. "Completely bloody butchered. It's like . . . it's like . . . "

"It's like we was in a meat factory," the sergeant said. "They're rashers, that's what they are; just so many bleeding rashers."

"There's a book on the table," the young man said. "A Mrs Beeton."

"So what?"

"Well, it's open at the bit about bacon. Almost as though . . . "

The sergeant, still dazed, took a notebook out of his pocket.

"Mother of God," he said without reverence.

P.C. Bates lifted his head with a sharp sideways movement, suddenly alert.

"I thought you'd been upstairs," he said. "Who's that laughing, then?"

122

# The Tigers Who Didn't Eat Meat

IT CAME about a long time ago that a small portion of the mainland of India was detached from that great continent by an insignificant but locally disruptive earthquake. The island so formed was but a few square miles in area, and fortunately for the plausibility of this story it contained a large number of trees bearing fruits and nuts, and a copious supply of constant cold water.

The formation of the island took place long before the advent of the species man, which is again just as well for the probability of what I have to relate. Indeed, almost the only sentient creatures it contained at the moment of division were a variety of birds, numerous deer, a pack of wolves, half a dozen antelope, an uncertain quantity of hares, a good many hogs, several hyenas, some sheep, and no-one could say how many smaller animals such as bandicoot-rats and other rodents. Of snakes and insects we need say nothing, save that they were far in excess of what even the most dedicated ecologist could consider essential.

I said "*almost* the only sentient creatures" for good reason, because it so happened that a pair of tigers was also trapped on this sudden ark of nature. Contrary to the belief of many, tigers are to be found even to this day not only in the mountains of India, but also in the low-lying swamp-lands that cover so much of that continent.

Tigers being what they are, this was a rotten stroke of fate for the other inhabitants of the island, for needless to

123

say the tigers lost no time in establishing the pecking order. The decimation took time, of course, as all species tend to breed when they get the chance. But the tigers multiplied as well, and unfortunately the original balance of population was so much in their favour that over a period of relatively few years the deer and the antelope, the wolves and hyenas, the hares et cetera, dwindled almost to nothing, while the tigers, being Top Animals in any jungle hierarchy, increased by leaps and gulps.

The day came, however, that the ecological facts of life caught up with the tigers, which is another way of saying that they ran out of grub. Not that grub in its widest sense was lacking. All around and above the stomach-rumbling tigers were trees laden with succulent citrus fruits, the ubiquitous mango, coconuts by the thousand, and any number of other products of a bountiful nature, many of them at ground level in the form of juicy shoots and inviting berries. But tigers are almost as thick-headed as our own species, so they regarded the island as barren. (But tolerance, please. The tiger was intended by nature to be carnivorous. Like most carnivora and omnivora he has a short bowel for the rapid expulsion of toxic food, jaws which close vertically with little or no lateral movement, long teeth and retractable claws for killing and holding his prey, and other physiological features that distinguish him sharply from the herbivorous and frugivorous species such as elephants, horses and the higher apes).

Fortunately for them and this story, the Leading Tiger was intellectually a bit ahead of the rest, and this combined with the instinct for survival led him one day to stay his paw from its intended destruction of the island's last remaining bandicoot as that rather charmless rodent was toying with a fallen mango. For it flashed into the tiger's mind – made sharper, perhaps, by the first pangs of starvation – that if a bandicoot could look so plump and self-satisfied on a diet of fruit, why not a tiger too? (In point of

124

fact, the bandicoot is omnivorous rather than frugivorous, but the tiger could not be expected to know that, and it is neither here nor there in any case).

As he ate the bandicoot (for once a predator, always a predator), the Leading Tiger thought some more, and the upshot was that by example and argument he convinced the rest of the tigers that they should henceforth adopt a diet centred on T.V.P., or Tigers' Vegetable Protein. And adopt they did. Fruits, nuts, shoots, leaves, berries, roots – you name it, those tigers ate it. And at first they *hated* so rigorous a change in their life-style. And can one blame them? For a vegetarian diet is not natural to a carnivore any more than is a diet of flesh to the Upper Primates, of which you and I, whether we like it or not, are fully paid up members.

However, one can get used to anything; but the tigers had particular trouble weaning their cubs, some of whom threw high-chair tantrums when faced with yukky dollops of mango or a branch of boring old leaves; for the young of all species resist food for which their guts are not designed.

The years passed, as is their habit. Nature ensured that the trees and plants continued to bear, and perhaps because an unnatural diet reduced the virility of their community, so keeping down their numbers, the tigers were able to support themselves after a fashion without even running out of food. Indeed, this was hardly surprising, seeing that much larger societies can be supported on plant foods than on the corpses of those who have consumed them.

But although they did not realise it, the tigers were a sick bunch of quadrupeds, and even those who were not incapacitated by actual diseases brought on by dietetic deficiencies were nevertheless functioning at a much lower level, physically and mentally, than when they were proud carnivores living off the captive flesh on the island. And their flatulence had to be heard to be believed.

125

So more years passed. And with their passage the tigers established a moderately workable compromise with their surroundings, although certain diseases were now endemic, and their energies and mental faculties were not a patch on what they used to be.

Came one day when the quite narrow channel between the island and the mainland was narrowed by a huge fall of rock, and the gap between became bridged by a large tree; for nature can be a dab hand at alternative technology when she puts her mind to it. The tigers were by now too lacking in initiative and intelligence to see the opportunity that had been given to them, so for some time life on the island continued as before. Then the moment arrived that a band of bandicoots, foraging among the flatsam on the foreshore of the mainland, scrabbled their way along the tree trunk and in all too short a time had established a colony. For bandicoots, like humans, rabbits and other "vermin", are alarmingly philo-progenitive.

Somewhat to the astonishment of the bandicoots, the tigers left them to their own devices and made no attempt to eat them. This was entirely satisfactory to the bandicoots, who soon became fat, lazy and trustful, and for a long while life on the island was an Eden-like routine of peaceful co-existence and general contentment.

But it was not to last. One of the tigers, in the course of munching despondently on its seven hundred and thirty third mango, consumed a small rodent that had hidden in the half-chewed fruit and gone to sleep. This taste of unaccustomed blood, while not particularly appealing to the tiger after a lifetime of realising the gastronomic ambitions of a orang-utan, nevertheless prompted a faint atavistic twinge in whatever part of his make-up such feelings are experienced.

All might have been well and as before had not a fat and unwary bandicoot happened to swagger past at that very moment. Standing as he was to loo'ard of the bandicoot, the tiger caught a whiff of that corpulent

126

omnivore, whose problem of personal freshness was not inconsiderable, and somehow it seemed to tie up with the last mouthful of rodent-laced mango and make some sort of crude sense . . .

At this point in this rather unpleasant story I must with reluctance fall back on the somewhat outworn device of anthropomorphism, which for the benefit of the peasants means I shall put human words into the mouths of the tigers. (On reflection, it is foolish to apologise for this. Tigers undoubtedly communicate with each other, as do all species, and since I do not understand their language I might as well ascribe to them a knowledge of ours).

To continue, then, it was some time before the tigers realised that one of their members had become a flesh-eater. But the day came when the gossip began, as it does in every community.

"Have you heard? Old Rumble was seen yesterday with the tail of a bandicoot hanging out of his mouth! He admitted to having eaten the creature!"

"A bandicoot! Disgusting! The animal must be a pervert."

"Bandicoot? You'll never see *me* eating such a thing. And what if the children took to the habit? Cubs need plenty of crisp coconuts and fresh ripened fruit if they are to build healthy teeth and bones."

"Well, now I look back, you know, I never did feel he was quite – well, one of *us*."

And there was a good deal of head-wagging and tail-swishing, for we are all wiser after the event.

But old Rumble was not to be the only defector. He had a wife and children, and while not all heads of families succeed in convincing their relations of the case for departing from habit, old Rumble had a time-honoured method for dealing with an argumentative spouse. After a few clips across her muzzle, Rumble's mate was not slow to start taking it out on the bandicoots. And anyway, after the first few mouthfuls she decided that bandicoot was no

127

end nicer than mango and coconut. And her flatulence improved immeasurably – by which I mean it got less.

But habits die hard, especially those centred on the stomach, and although bandicoot is undoubtedly natural, walking tiger-food, the vast majority of the tigers on the island continued to eat mango and coconut and to feel off-colour and flatulate and die before their time. And perhaps because deep in their collective unconscious they knew that at some point in time past they had taken a wrong turning, or perhaps because the meat-eating section was clearly healthier and more energetic than they were, they resented the flesh-golloping minority and in no time had invented a wide range of rude names with which to label them (for if there is one good way of getting an uncomfortable idea into perspective, it is to label it rudely). One of these names was, in tiger language, Craaaaank, and before long this became abbreviated and passed into common use.

So that was how things went. Gastronomically and socially (for the two are closely linked) the tigers remained in separate camps. The tigers who didn't eat meat had as little as possible to do with those that did, and those that did just got on with it and didn't lose much sleep about those that didn't. For while those that did were called "cranks" and a lot of other cubbish names, they instinctively knew that the mango-eating tigers, although numerically superior, were themselves the cranky ones, for anyone who eats the food that nature intended for other species and scorns the food intended for his own is surely as cranky as anything you could mention.

To-day, of course, all the tigers on the island eat meat and are as fit as fiddles. Just how this came about, history does not relate. Maybe the tigers who didn't eat meat were eventually converted by those who did, if only because those who did were fitter and lived longer and more fully than those who didn't. Or maybe those who did eat meat multiplied so rapidly that once again the other in-

128

habitants of the island ran out, figuratively speaking, leaving the meat-eating tigers no alternative to consuming their weaker brethren. Either way it was a case of conversion – in a sense.

As for what it all goes to prove, this will be obvious only to those with the eyes to see, the ears to hear, and stomachs that are as receptive to common-sense as their open minds.

# Mrs Widdowes' Speculation

At that stage no-one could have known that the teddy bears were going to decide the matter.

"But as well as starting a dancing school," Mrs Widdowes said, trying to sound businesslike, "I would want to live there."

The estate agent inflated his cheeks. A florid man, he seemed to find even seated conversation taxing. His mid-morning breath suggested recent celebration, and Mrs Widdowes wondered if she should have gone to one of the town's larger firms.

"No problem," he puffed. "The place has light-industrial use as well as shop, office and residential."

"And you say the room I could use for my school has been a workshop?"

She knew she must be quite clear about the planning position. "With the bureaucratic mind," her husband had always said, "you can't be too careful." She was missing that unimaginative competence with which he had sheltered her from so many of the worries and negotiations of modern life.

"For close on two centuries," the agent assured her. "It was one of the oldest businesses in the town until Mr Kneebone died."

"What type of business?" Mrs Widdowes enquired.

The agent hesitated. "A service trade." He waved a hand, as though dismissing a point of no relevance, then flicked an unseen fly from his lapel.

Mrs Widdowes was more concerned about the financial aspect.

"Of course, I've the mortgage to pay off on our . . . my present house before selling, but I suppose I'd have just enough. It doesn't *sound* expensive."

"A bargain. An executors' sale."

"And Mrs Kneebone lived there until she died?"

"Right! The place was never out of her family's hands. You may find the residential portion a little primitive as a consequence, but the charm and potentialities won't escape you." He handed her a key. "Oh! And don't mind the bears."

"Bears?"

"The house is empty except for a quantity of toy bears. Mrs Kneebone collected them, it seems. Maybe something to do with her having no family. They were left behind when the place was cleared; for fear of moth, no doubt."

"I shan't mind teddy bears at all," Mrs Widdowes said. Childless herself, she saw nothing strange in Mrs Kneebone's hobby. "I'd be much more worried by mice."

Except that the sills to the small, grimy casements had almost rotted away, and that the bow-fronted window to the office end of the ground floor was painfully modern, the passing years could have seen little change. Slate-roofed and cobble-walled, the cottage was square and dumpy, crouching apologetically below the blank cliffs of the new office blocks whose fenestration disdained an outlook across so humble a reminder of the passing character of the small cathedral city. Its south and east boundaries were a tall brick and flint wall, creeper covered, giving privacy to the ground floor. From the broken gate in the wall a short path led to the narrow green front door. The crooked lintel above it was explained by the crack in the cobbled wall it supported. Even more cracks were apparent in the cement covering most of the narrow area that had once been garden. Through the cracks marigolds and honesty had grown, adding in their decay to the autumnal rubbish of spent weeds and the tin and paper reminders of the town's summer visitors. In one corner Mrs Widdowes noticed a pile of stone chippings of different colours and textures, mixed in with wood-shavings and sawdust.

What she noticed most of all was how still it was behind the high-rise blocks. The cottage seemed encapsulated in undisturbed air, as though its life had been held in colourless amber since invasion by the surrounding symbols of civic progress.

She paused before trying her key in the lock, picturing the cottage when its setting had been trees, hollyhocks and sunflowers. The agent had been right about the charm, even though this owed more to nostalgia than to present appearance. It was perhaps an awareness of the transitory nature of things – even those as solid as flint and slate – that sent a quick, cold tremor down her spine. Or possibly it was the contemplation of anything as serious as house purchase without her husband's rigid but comforting authority to fall back upon. She had not welcomed the liberation that came with widowhood.

The crude iron key turned harshly but easily in the lock. Standing in the agents' "small entrance vestibule", Mrs Widdowes found that without moving a step from its centre she could close the front door behind her, reach out to the doors on either side, or put her hand on the stair rail in front. The door on the right, saying "Office", was modern and flat-surfaced with a restrained but contemporary lever handle. The door opposite, six-panelled and much older, had a plain porcelain finger plate and knob. She knew it must lead into the workshop.

Deciding to start at the top, Mrs Widdowes climbed the stairs; and "climb" was the fitting verb. The stairs were narrow and steep, and the wobbling wallrail that was no more than a fat broom handle worn shiny with the friction of generations of hands, gave little sense of security. Two of the treads gave soggily to the pressure of her feet, and

132

she made her way to the small, rickety landing nervously, imposing as little of her weight on each stair as possible.

The narrow landing supported the agents' assertion of simplicity and compactness. To left and right were simple latched doors, their thick cream paint bearing the grime and vertical cracks of extreme and little-tended age. She opened the right-hand door. The room, no more than eighteen feet by ten, was empty except for an urn-shaped green tin vase on the narrow windowsill, and the end nearest the door had been given a crude division, creating the "en suite" bathroom that added substance to the admission that "some modernisation may be desirable." She turned the worn cold tap in the small corner washbasin. It spurted a half cup of brown water, gurgled weakly, then died with a falling hiss.

Until she opened the door to the room opposite, Mrs Widdowes had forgotten about the teddy bears. Because the window was small and dirty, and the day overcast, she did not see them immediately, being more concerned whether the floorboards would support her. But the old oak planks, although uneven and gappy, were sound. More instantly apparent was the silence of the room. The outside world of traffic and people might have been miles away. She stood quite still for a moment and thought about the silence, deciding it must be due to the solid walls and the surrounding buildings.

Then she saw the teddy bears, which is to say she took them in for what they were rather than as an unidentified background to her thoughts about floorboards and silence. They were hardly to be overlooked. The whole of the wall in front of her was occupied by them, filling four or five tiers of shelving, each bear sitting close to its neighbour, eyes fixed on the inner wall through whose door she had entered.

In the moment of recognition, Mrs Widdowes gave a little gasp. It is not an everyday experience to meet the unblinking gaze of some two hundred teddy bears. Then

133

she smiled and felt the small, warm feeling we all experience when encountering the more comforting symbols of our childhoods. Her eyes ranged along each shelf in turn, taking in the slight absurdity of the hundreds of bare and sometimes worn feet pads that seemed to be inviting her inspection. With the illogic we reserve for things that touch our hearts, she was sorry the bears were so shabby and forgotten. She took one down off its shelf and blew some of the dust from the top of its head. It lacked one eye and an arm and was almost bald, but it had the air of an animal that had received inordinate love over a long period. Another – a large bear with eyes a shade too closely set to be called handsome – reminded her of her own Mr Honey who had lasted into her early middle age, surviving the slow corruption of moth, dust and long devotion, but having no defence against the pair of attic mice who eventually raised a large and incontinent family in its stomach.

Mrs Widdowes replaced the bear and tried to think about practicalities. The ceiling was far from level, but she told herself that if it had stayed up for so many years, there was no logical reason to suppose it would descend in a choking cloud of dust as soon as she had taken possession. The wallpaper had been painted over, but seemed good for further coats, despite some lifting along the seams. As for woodworm and rot, she decided sensibly that it would be best to assume that both were rampant rather than to go round looking for them.

Then, all of a sudden, she wanted to leave the room, for there was something about the silent, unblinking teddy bears – perhaps the sheer quantity – that made her feel almost an intruder. Yet the immobile silence of the forsaken toys had somehow moved her, and as she left the room she looked back at them with a half smile.

"I suppose I should have it surveyed before deciding. It will take every penny I have, and small dancing schools are not very profitable. It will be a very speculative venture."

The agent's gesture heralded the onset of a favour.

"It is not normal practice, but I think I can tell you that another lady was interested in the house, but died suddenly before completion. She lent me a copy of her surveyor's report. If you would care to take it away with you . . ."

Perhaps because she was already some way toward making up her mind, Mrs Widdowes felt he had her interests at heart.

"That's very kind of you! Certainly you were right about the workshop. It would do very well. But the whole place needs quite a lot spent on it."

"A fact reflected in the price," he said quickly. His professional instinct for the serious purchaser was prompting a more cheerful confidence.

"Well, I would certainly like to see the report," said Mrs Widdowes. "I am most grateful."

"All part of the service," the agent said, smiling a rare smile.

When she went to sleep that night, and when she woke up, Mrs Widdowes was thinking about the cottage. More exactly, she was thinking about the workshop and the teddy bears, but more about the teddy bears than the workshop, which as she told herself more than once was not really relevant. The predicament of two hundred abandoned bears was assuming proportions that her own reason told her were ridiculous. Nevertheless, it was the bears that were on her mind when she arrived at the agent's office.

"Are they included?" she asked anxiously, a chair having been accepted and the weather agreed upon.

The agent stopped studying a note he had found about covenants and looked up questioningly.

"The bears," Mrs Widdowes explained.

135

"Included?" For a moment he wondered if she was using the bears as a lever to get the price down, but her face told him otherwise. "Do you mean you want them?"

Mrs Widdowes felt uncomfortable; a little ridiculous. But she replied firmly:

"Well, with a dancing class, and small children, homes might be found . . ."

Estate agents are men who acquire a wide experience of the unpredictability of human ambitions and failings.

"Ah, yes, of course!" His tone suggested total affinity with the trend of her reasoning. "Well, I shall certainly see if that can be arranged. I anticipate no difficulty. Now there is this question of joint access to the rear of the property . . ."

"Yes, of course," Mrs Widdowes said, leaning forward eagerly in her chair, her face showing collaborative intent, her mind filled with matters ursine.

"What is more," said the agent, who by now had seen where his client's priorities lay, "it is all right about the bears."

"In that case," said Mrs Widdowes, her head swimming slightly, "I am ready to sign the contract to-morrow. I can be in Mr Slocum's office first thing in the morning."

"Excellent! He will have left by now, but I shall ring him before ten."

"Do you mind if I go round now and do a little measuring? There are some wall mirrors coming up in a sale to-morrow, and they might just do."

"Certainly! But will you have enough light?"

"There is a bulb in the workshop, which is all I shall need."

As she walked the few hundred yards to the cottage, Mrs Widdowes found that momentous happenings really can produce a slightly tipsy, feet-off-the-ground feeling. With a down-to-earth husband taking the initiative throughout an uneventful marriage, she had never before tasted the heady effects of independently arrived-at decisions on the grand scale.

She was approaching the cottage when the street lamp on the other side of the road flickered and held steady. It was an orange, colour-draining light, as functional as the concrete stem that carried it, reducing the healthiest of human complexions to a level of cadaverous finality.

The recent rain must have swollen the front door, for it resisted the pressure of her hand and creaked protestingly. Before entering the workshop, Mrs Widdowes measured the bow window; coming almost down to floor level, it would need a lot of nylon curtaining.

The cottage's only bulb could have been no more than a 40 watt. It made the workshop look dingier than ever, adding to the dusk's inbuilt depression. Drawing a deep, positive breath, Mrs Widdowes began to take measurements. The mirrors, she decided, would fill the area between wall and cupboard nicely.

The cupboard, some five feet wide, was a fixture. It bore the air of advanced age but with none of the attraction of antiquity. Its doors were fastened by two staples and a piece of wire which Mrs Widdowes undid. The shelves held nothing but a few screws, three jam jars and a waxy cloth.

The cupboard stopped short of the ceiling. Expecting the dirt of years, Mrs Widdowes felt gingerly along the top. Her fingers met the edge of something. It seemed to be a board – an extra shelf for the cupboard, she thought – and she eased it gently towards her, narrowing her eyes as dust and grime descended. The end of the board, which was too short to be a shelf, had a vaguely familiar shape, and had she taken it down and examined it she might have been startled to see it was the lid of a small coffin. As it was, she pushed it back and brushed her fingers, anxious to resume her measuring.

When she had finished, Mrs Widdowes' mind turned to the floor above, and thinking about the floor above led naturally to thinking about the bears. The prospect of

137

becoming their owner was a pleasant one. She had already made up her mind that whatever might be best for the remainder, she would keep the one she thought of as Mr Honey's brother. She decided to go up and see they were all right before she left the cottage.

The front door was too modest to be topped by a fanlight, so the staircase was almost in darkness as she groped her way to the landing. When she entered the bears' room she was relieved that the street lamp gave enough light to pick her way across the uneven floor to the just discernible toys. Once again the dead stillness of the room struck her, and she shivered a little. Stillness and a slight chill reactivated that sense of removal and isolation from a world that was neither heard nor heeding.

Mrs Widdowes peered fondly at Mr Honey's brother. If he was really of the same age, his preservation was quite remarkable. She remembered that Mr Honey had had a yellow manufacturer's label sewn into the top of his back seam. If his brother had the same . . .

She took the bear off its shelf, blew some of the dust off its face, rubbed the slightly loose glass eyes, and turned it over in her hand, moving to the window to make use of the street lamp's baleful gleam. There *was* a label, but not sewn into the seam. It was a faded paper label, merely stuck to the bear's hair-thin back at what could inexactly be called waist level.

Mrs Widdowes peered at the worn writing, but it defeated her naked eye. She rummaged in her handbag for her reading glasses, then manoeuvred the toy until its label received maximum illumination. It was still not easy to make out. The first line was in capital letters.

She spelled them out, slowly and half aloud: "S . . . T . . . E . . . Oh! Stephen! S . . . H . . . A . . . W. Stephen Shaw!"

It seemed an odd name for a bear. But there was more writing on the label and it was some time before she made sense of it. It was in normal hand-writing, not capitals,

138

and rather wobbly as if done by someone elderly or under stress.

"Here," she read out slowly, "is Edward Bear, dar . . . ling. He will never forget you, nor will we. Your loving mummy and daddy."

It was not until she had deciphered the final line, more faintly written in pencil by another hand, that Mrs Widdowes' understanding went beyond mere identification of the words. The last line was short and to the point:

"Born 1st May 1973. Died 22nd December 1980."

As though jig-saw pieces had suddenly found their places in her sub-conscious mind, Mrs Widdowes remembered the coffin-ended plank and related it to this confirmation of a child's short span of life. She recalled the agent's evasive response when she asked about Mr Kneebone's business.

"Oh, no!" Mrs Widdowes whispered, aghast. "Not an undertakers!"

For a moment she stood motionless, the bear in her hand, her head still tilted to catch the light on the label, but her eyes unseeing. Then she pulled herself together with a shake of the head and went quickly to the shelves, replaced Mr Honey's brother, and took another toy from a little further along. It, too, had a label stuck to its back. The writing was stronger, and by the light of the street lamp she had less difficulty making out the typed words:

"Belinda Martin born January 27th 1988, died 3rd March 1993."

Feverishly Mrs Widdowes replaced the bear and took others down from their shelves. In most cases the labels were intact and the essential details the same. Not all had messages, but on every one the dates were given and seldom spanned more than the few years of a brief childhood.

"She *couldn't*," Mrs Widdowes said half aloud, an hysterical note in her voice, "she couldn't have robbed the

139

coffins of their *bears!*"

But in her heart she knew what Mrs Kneebone had done, and in her heart she identified, horribly if briefly, with the childless despair and emptiness of a woman she would never know.

The moan that escaped her was compounded of rage, pity and an unfamiliar kind of fear; reluctant acceptance gave way to an overwhelming distress. The tears that came were strong and angry, so violent that they misted her spectacles, and as she removed them with the reflex intention of wiping them clean it seemed that her moan of dismay and realisation was being taken up and echoed by the confronting rows of dusty toys.

By some trick of the street lamp, perhaps, the eyes of some of the teddy bears appeared to be flashing and darting at her, and what had begun as a slight rising and falling wail was now punctuated by shrill, protesting squeals, grunts and growls – pathetic, impotent sounds of distress and fury.

Mrs Widdowes backed away from the shelves, nearly falling as she caught her heel between uneven boards. Her thin shoulder blades met the opposite wall. The eyes of the teddy bears were now like a battery of tiny, probing, vengeful searchlights, eating into her with seeming hatred and defiance. Yet in the screams and growls was an occasional note that was as much a plea as a threat, as suggestive of despair as of loathing.

Without being able to take her eyes from the dim but clamorous shelves, Mrs Widdowes edged along the wall, feeling with her right hand for the door. Puzzlement, pity and anger no longer dominated. She was governed by only one emotion and only one intent: terror and escape.

Her hand found the door and she felt her way on to the landing above the steep stairs, groping for the rickety hand rail that might lead a calm and cautious person to the front door below and the other world beyond.

140

# A Walk Across The Fields

THE PATH across the fields was muddy from the February rains. Turf is frail in winter, its dormant roots too weak to grasp wet soil, too indifferent to life's struggle to make repair. Feet and bicycle tyres punished the path daily, for it was a convenient short cut from Clifton Grange to the village half a mile away.

It was not an uplifting day. The flat lands of Bedfordshire, in that area seldom free from the pungent reminder of growing cabbage, did little to raise the spirits, even in the best of weather. On this day the wind was keen, though less biting than it had been, and the woman sensed the promise of rain.

She turned and called the child to hurry, anxious to deliver her parcel to the post office and to be back in time for lunch. Had the weather been more tempting they would have left earlier and gone the other way, walking down the long drive whose chestnut trees canopied with their bare branches the carpet of snowdrops and aconites. But the child would have wanted to test the frozen water that lay, not quite a pond but more than a puddle, among the trees on the north side of the drive.

The boy had stopped, his legs apart, his feet planted firmly on the path. He was gazing stolidly at the ground between his wellington boots, preoccupied with something more compelling than familiar appeals concerning time and schedules.

"Now, come on, Peter." Miss Chamberlain's voice did

not hold expectation of instant obedience.

She looked back at the grange and its surrounding straggle of smaller buildings and walls. To the left of the main house she could see the tiled roof of the cottage she and the boy had for their own use. It had been converted from the stables when the grange became a residential hotel, and it was separated from the house by a walled yard, containing in one corner an oak tree that must have predated it by some hundreds of years.

In the cottage, consisting of two small rooms, Miss Chamberlain and her charge slept, lived, and for the most part ate their meals. It was not the normal arrangement in those early between-wars years for a nanny to be involved in the preparation of food, but time had established an understanding between herself and Mrs Etherington that gave room to such special concessions without fear of friction. It was an understanding based on respect. Miss Chamberlain fully accepted that her employer – though without any loss of respect she found it difficult to think of Mrs Etherington in that capacity – needed to observe a rigid and closely guarded daily routine if she was to continue to write her novels. For although she could see that Mollie Etherington's books were a little "strong" in places, she applauded warmly their moral messages of a fervour and sincerity amounting at times to exhortation. Of an earlier generation, Miss Chamberlain approved highly of such an unequivocal stance in an era showing all too many signs of ethical decline.

"Peter! Come *along*! It is about to rain."

Without raising his head the child pointed at the mud between his feet, his arm and index finger a straight line of absorbed enquiry.

His nurse retraced her steps, a shade impatiently, and stared at the ground sternly, a little as though daring it to justify the child's procrastination.

"That, do you mean?"

She pointed with her foot at the black rubber heel,

impressed with the pattern of a star, and doubtless lost from some worn boot.

Peter nodded slowly, awaiting explanation, anchored by concentration.

Miss Chamberlain suffered from only the most infrequent bursts of imagination. Given – one might say dedicated – to telling the truth, she seldom indulged in flights of fancy. Stories about gnomes and fairies were one thing; the imaginative treatment of day to day actualities quite another.

But the stoutest character can be caught off guard. With rain threatening and the post office near to lunchhour closing, Miss Chamberlain permitted herself a moment of artistic licence.

"When a star has fallen, you cannot put it back."

As though that put the matter to rest, she held out her hand, inviting the speed that comes with borrowed power.

Her invitation was not taken up. The child continued to gaze at the heel, his forehead registering perplexity. At length he looked up at her, his face beneath the wide brim of his grey felt hat serious and intent.

"Stars," he pointed out firmly, "are all shiny."

Already regretting her lapse, Miss Chamberlain hesitated, anxious that the boy should not build on her small deceit. Marrying relevance to trust, she said:

"When a star falls, it burns in the air. Then it goes black, just like a coal that drops out of the grate."

She took his arm and pulled him to her side, with the knowledge that diverted attention is usually the best answer to difficult questions. So great was his concentration on the matter in hand that his feet responded simultaneously, so that he swung half round before submitting to the necessity to walk.

"Look!" Miss Chamberlain invited, "there's Charlie."

Charlie was a broken-winged crow they often met when crossing the fields. As usual, the bird allowed Peter to come almost within touching distance before hopping just

143

out of reach, one bright eye judging the child's intentions without fear. She took Peter's hand again.

"Now we *really* must get along," Miss Chamberlain said.

The progress of Miss Chamberlain under full sail was an event that repaid study, brooking no hindrance, and developed from many years' experience of the preferred pace of small children. Her clothing emphasized the aura of unquestionable majesty. Although the second quarter of the century was well established, her outdoor wear was buttoned, businesslike and plain, of a style Edwardian more than post-war. Grey as befitted her station, it was topped by a warm cloak with a purple lining. Her head was crowned, as always, by a capacious hat whose size was hardly justified by the quantity of greying hair she had to put into it. Nor was its formidableness a whit diminished by being impaled with steel pins of a size and variety of direction that reminded cultivated observers of one of the more graphic portrayals of the martyrdom of Saint Sebastian.

Familiarity with Miss Chamberlain could never have bred contempt, but the very young have reasonable reserves of rebellion. Peter began to pull.

"Come along, dear," Miss Chamberlain said, her head not turning nor her pace slackening.

The boy ran forward a few steps, then jumped, digging his heels into the soft ground and leaning back as Miss Chamberlain's progress took up the slack in their joined arms. It was a determined move, at least enough to register serious intention.

"Now, *Peter!*"

Miss Chamberlain came to a halt with a half turn, rather as a boat will do in a following wind when its mooring rope is made fast before the sails are lowered.

"Want to go back," Peter said resolutely, "and get it."

"Get what, dear?" his nurse asked impatiently, her mind fixed on parcels, closing times, and impending lunch.

144

"The star. I want the star."

"You can't have a dirty thing like that. Mummy would not want you to."

The child's mouth took on the tremulous firmness that precedes tears.

"Now, Peter, you know the post office closes early."

Rebellion was invariably short-lived. The tone of Miss Chamberlain's voice left no doubt that the boy had already pushed his luck a good deal further than could be considered reasonable and fitting. His nurse and mother, seemingly in constant touch with God's will, were a combined force whose moral strength was more than any mortal of barely five years could reasonably contend with. Although the cold of the day could not alone have accounted for his watering eyes, Peter allowed his progress to be boosted by Miss Chamberlain's masterful arm.

They reached the post office just as Mr Rogerson was about to turn the key. His wife, who managed the general stores without which the post office side would have provided no living, and vice versa, had called him for his lunch.

"I am sorry to arrive so near to your closing time, Mr Rogerson," Miss Chamberlain said, the regret in her voice modified by that regality common to professional nannies whose long service to a number of good families made them well aware of life's pecking order, "but we were a little delayed. By one thing or another," she added, looking down at Peter with a touch of severity.

Mr Rogerson felt no resentment. Lunch was to be leftovers of a meal he had not much enjoyed the day before, and in any case it would have made no sense to offend anyone who came from Clifton Grange. The Grange was the Rogerson's largest single account, quite excluding the individual residents who came to them for life's secondary incidentals such as toothpaste and chocolate.

"Rain on the way," Mr Rogerson promised, stamping the parcel.

"As I told Master Peter," Miss Chamberlain agreed complacently, separating her charge from the Rogerson's collie before his pleasure in renewing acquaintance with the animal led to a licked face and hands. Peter loved animals and felt no fear of them, whatever their size and disposition. His nurse had no conscious wish to destroy whatever satisfaction might be had from such sources, but her passion for hygiene was equalled only by the desire shared with Peter's mother for moral rectitude.

"And we could do with a little butter," she added. "Four ounces should be just enough to be going on with."

She had a deep faith in the virtues of small quantities. Almost every substance capable of division was judged as of higher merit if it arrived in portions that were just enough to be going on with.

Mr Rogerson dipped his butter pats into water and clipped a wedge of best salted English from the large round that stood on the comparative coolness of the marble slab. His Scotch hands, as he called the pats, were of finest boxwood, and he was quite aware that his technique was well developed.

His expert patting and moulding of the lump was enough to reconcile Peter to separation from the dog, for the child always watched the process with great concentration and enjoyment.

"And now," said Miss Chamberlain, as the Rogerson's door was closed behind them, "we must just go round to Mitchell's to see if we can find a nice bit of fish. A little piece of plaice will do very well for our supper."

It was a familiar statement. Every Friday Miss Chamberlain sought out a nice bit of fish, and her choice was invariably a little piece of plaice. Once, when the spots were not red enough to guarantee freshness, they had made do with a dab, but by the time the fish had been cooked slowly in milk, with a nut of butter and a shake of pepper, the difference in flavour was neither here nor there.

146

Peter was not fond of the fishmonger's clammy shop. The glassy, given-up stare of the lifeless, slimy creatures was bad enough, but the eye-level view he had into the blood-red, fanned-out gills of the larger fish that had expired at half gasp, affected him more. Even worse, Mr Mitchell kept a shallow dish of live eels, and on one occasion another customer's order had resulted in a be-heading and division he had since dreaded seeing repeated. Whether pity or fear prompts such reactions in the very young, poses a distinction difficult to determine in later life; whatever the spur, Peter's reactions to such events did not weaken with familiarity.

He was perhaps fortunate that his mother and nurse were women of the best possible intentions. Neither would have set out to suppress or condemn any emotional or mental response that seemed natural, wholesome or reasonable. The small and usually physical things, like fingers up noses, were of course discouraged, and alter-natives strongly recommended; but it is doubtful whether these are often the issues that produce those traumata later recognised with such confidence by the psychiatrists. Temper and grief were accepted by Miss Chamberlain – though with rather less equanimity by Peter's mother – as normal reactions to life's unavoidable vicissitudes. But to both women the greater – they might have said higher – importance lay in the positive rather than negative approach. That is to say, they shared the deeply felt belief that by focusing on whatever things were true, honest, just, pure, lovely and of good report, there would be a steadily receding need to keep harmony and order by repression, prohibition and punishment. Needless to say, in such situations much depends upon what is regarded as repression, prohibition and punishment, but it has to be admitted that by their subscription to disciplines of Absolute Truth (Mrs Etherington favoured capitals for all the most important concepts) they tended to be relent-lessly, some would have said maddeningly, right.

So Miss Chamberlain did not attempt to eliminate Peter's reactions to the fishmonger's dismal wares by those accusations of silliness or misbehaviour commonly employed to instill into the young that insensitivity that avoids complication or embarrassment in later life. Rather, she concentrated her energies on ensuring that Mr Mitchell filleted the chosen fish out of sight behind his counter while Peter's attention was drawn to whatever nearby event might help to fend off association between the white substance he would have for supper and the flabby corpse on a slab. For while Miss Chamberlain subscribed genuinely enough to the view that healthy emotions should not be repressed, she saw no point in inviting pointless provocation. In this respect she was more diplomatic than Mrs Etherington, whose reactions to almost everything were instant and unmistakable.

"And now," she said, when the uninspiring object of so much forward planning was wrapped in a lurid page from The Daily Mirror and safely in her waterproof shopping bag, "we must get home before the skies fall."

It was not the wisest simile to have chosen.

"Can we get the star, Nana?"

Miss Chamberlain sighed. She had forgotten the rubber heel.

"We shall have to hurry if we are not to be caught in the rain," she said.

It was not quite a "no", so Peter let it go at that.

They headed for home at what Miss Chamberlain deemed a "smart pace," which is to say that Peter trotted three steps for every one he walked. And then an errand boy, whistling home to lunch, his hands contemptuous of the need to steer his bicycle, made a face at him. It was so involved and enigmatic a contortion, and emanating from so dashing a source, that Peter's next few moments were spent in the happy oblivion of emulation, until his nurse shook his arm and warned, with a measure of sincerity, that if he wasn't careful he would get stuck like that.

148

Peter could see no reason for fearing so promising a fate, but for the sake of a quiet life he allowed his experiments to fade away slowly in a brief canter of modified grimaces and twitches.

There was a short cut from the fishmonger's to the lane that led across the fields, and it ran alongside a red brick wall, three times at least the height of Miss Chamberlain. There were gates in the wall, which was topped by savage pieces of broken glass, while the gates themselves bore iron spikes that reminded Peter of the Prussian helmets in one of his picture books. Perhaps because of the shadow cast by so tall a structure, it always seemed cooler and more dismal in that part of the village, and Peter never resisted his nurse's tendency at that point to hurry him along. On this day, under a sky grey and misty with impending rain, the urge to dawdle was even weaker than usual.

The first warning drops began to fall as they passed the brown-painted gates, and Miss Chamberlain was just about to say something that would have helped to cement in Peter's mind the accuracy of adult prediction, when the quiet of the lane was shattered by a sound so piercing and intense that it penetrated the thick timber with enough force for Miss Chamberlain herself to be stopped in her majestic tracks.

"Oh, dear!" she said, in a tone that acknowledged an event likely to produce a challenge not clearly susceptible of solution.

Peter, too, had stopped, the last experimental, face-saving twitch now replaced by a wide-eyed expression of such questioning anxiety that his nurse knew it would be best to anticipate the inevitable demand for explanation.

"It is just a pig, dear."

She felt instinctively that it was to be her most testing skirmish to date in that difficult area where a desire to speak nothing but the truth is inevitably at odds with the warmer urge to soften the hard facts that bewilder those

149

too young for the early pangs of sophistication.

"It is just a pig, dear," was not good enough, and they both knew it. "Just a pig", to Peter, was a beady-eyed, grunting animal whose familiarity with mud was seemingly unlimited, and whose pleasure at being scratched with a stick was something that could be shared wherever access to a sty might be offered by a friendly farmer.

The squealing continued. The mixture of fear and rage in the protests of an aroused pig can prompt the soundest nerves to crave an end to it. The end that Miss Chamberlain suspected was not one she wished Peter to know about. She was not a countrywoman by birth or upbringing, and aware that the wall surrounding the yard belonged to Mr Burgess, the village butcher and horse-knacker, she guessed that the end was to come by bullet or knife, and she wanted Peter out of earshot.

"Why is it crying?"

The child's face was tense and had lost some of its colour.

"Pigs are very quick to make a fuss about things," Miss Chamberlain replied, fighting inwardly a small contest that was becoming ever more familiar.

"Poor pig!"

The animal's protests were reaching a crescendo, or what might have been considered such in any species less prone to an almost unlimited range of vocal response to the injustices of a man-made world.

Miss Chamberlain pointed upward. "Here comes the rain!" she said with a cheerfulness out of keeping with her normal reaction to a threat of uninvited water on her charge or her hat. "We must hurry."

"But why?" Peter asked.

The question was clearly not provoked by the need for haste. Miss Chamberlain braced herself to put truth before evasion.

"I think they may be going to turn it into bacon."

If a hint of the miracles of fairyland had crept into her

150

voice, Mrs Etherington would have forgiven her.

Had she but known, Mr Burgess had no intention of slaughtering the pig for at least three weeks. It was merely being moved from pen to pen. But pigs being intelligent and sensitive creatures, capable of cheating the slaughterer by dying of fright alone, this particular animal was indifferent to the finer distinctions and was taking valid exception to being dragged by a rope through its snout.

Unaware that although right in her essential facts, the end that comes in sudden silence, or the gargling squeal of a warm-blooded creature drowning in its own blood, was not yet imminent, Miss Chamberlain tugged gently in the direction of home. But Peter was standing sideways on to his nurse, facing the gates, his legs wide apart, well positioned for resistance.

"Bacon?"

There were associations to be pondered. Bacon was what his parents ate for breakfast, though it was only at week-ends that Peter shared that meal with them.

Miss Chamberlain pulled with slow but steady determination until, almost without Peter being conscious of the fact, they were moving toward the lane, away from the pig's clamour. His mind was tussling with the problem of reconciling a live, grunting animal with the thin rashers of anonymous, aromatic food that seemed inseparable from his parents' first meal of the day.

The concept of death was not entirely new to him. More than a hint had been given by the weekly purchases at Mr Mitchell's; by the rabbits and game on hooks outside the butcher's shop; by a dead dog seen in the road beyond the drive. But the verb "to kill" had as yet come no closer than when one of the grange's cats had been playing with a mouse during the half hour that Peter's mother tried to spend with him before his bedtime. The cat had been squatting by the old stone water-trough, filled with geraniums, that stood on bricks a few feet from the cottage door. Peter had been delighted to witness the sense of fun between cat and mouse, the latter running again and again under the trough, only to be hooked out by the crouching cat's paw. Lacking children of his own age to play with, he enjoyed watching two animals inventing a game that reminded him of the rare occasions when his father found time to play "He". He had therefore been startled when his mother had exclaimed with concern and rushed at the cat, frightening it away from the mouse who this time scuttled to the shelter of the nearby timber garage that housed Flight Lieutenant Etherington's Wolsey. Only then, as his mother explained the cat's intentions, did Peter begin to understand that in life there are those whose pleasure depends on another's death.

But a child's interpretation of the world's motivation is a partial understanding. Peter's grasp of the reality took no account of the possibility that people – people like his parents and nurse – could themselves share such pleasure. The butcher's shop was still a phenomenon that held no firm link with himself or his family. It was a place whose hanging animals and birds were a meaningless exhibition without relevance to daily life, although instinctively he preferred to walk by on the other side of the street.

So Miss Chamberlain did not have an easy time of it as they walked back across the fields. Although her previous charges had also wanted assurances and explanations, their reconciliation to the harsher facts of life had been helped by a closer relationship with parents united in acceptance of the inevitability of nature red in tooth, claw and hand.

Miss Chamberlain saw, and did not resent, that it was she who bore the brunt of responsibility for the boy's development. Peter's father was stationed at Henlow, which was why they had taken rooms in a residential hotel, and his affair with a brother officer's wife had brought his marriage to the point where interest in his son's development was fitful and shallow. Lost in her writing, and herself an only child whose background had poorly prepared her for marriage and parental responsibility, Mollie Etherington's energies were devoted more to the vision of how life might one day be than to recognising any urgent need, or indeed means, of helping Peter to understand how, so unfortunately, it already was. On the occasions that she was able to detect the opportunity for such instruction, her methods relied more on shock from sudden outburst than on the gentler, more subtle devices innate in women with a better developed instinct for motherhood.

Miss Chamberlain could see from Peter's face that her explanations were too guarded or too preposterous to put his mind at rest. Faced with making a palatable package from irreconcilable factors, she was relieved when they reached the spot where Peter had found the heel. She greeted the discarded object almost as an old friend, even bending to dislodge it from the embracing mud.

"Well, there we are!" she exclaimed with a somewhat false delight. "It is still here after all."

The possibility of the heel having launched itself back into space, presumably brightening on its ascent, had not really been mooted, but in Miss Chamberlain's voice was relief at a whole range of fears unrealised.

Peter took the heel she held out to him, but his worried expression did not change to one of pleasure. He looked at the rubber object as though he had not seen it before, then with his free hand pulled his nurse's arm, now as anxious as she had been to return home.

Near the edge of the field they came across Charlie again, picking listlessly at the sparse offerings on the winter soil. But this time the bird flapped away from them, as though frightened by strangers; as though, Peter felt, they were no longer, almost, friends.

So they climbed the wooden stile, crossed the narrow paddock that fringed the southern boundary of the grange, and passed through the love-gate in the open iron railings that ran from the road end of the drive to the walled garden that was their destination.

As they crossed the grass verge bordering the drive, a gong summoned the grange's guests to lunch. Peter's mother, whose room was on the first floor overlooking the drive, was just visible behind the window, and as they reached the gravel she rose from her desk to give a little wave. Miss Chamberlain's response was a shade more eager than usual, but while Peter at her bidding looked up at the window, his smile was bleak and his arm rose hardly as high as his shoulder. Then the blur of his mother's figure was gone, and the deep peals of the gong died into silence.

"Now we must go and see what *we* can find for lunch," Miss Chamberlain said cheerfully. "How would you like one of those little fairy cakes for your pudding? With some bramble jelly?"

Peter nodded. They went through the open gateway into the yard, beneath the old oak. As they skirted the area of rough grass in the centre of the yard, a sweeping of fine rain blew in from the west, darkening the roofs and the gravel in the drive, softening the mud on the black rubber heel that lay on the verge in front of the grange.

The best of the day had gone.